"But I've always called you sir before."

"You've always been a brunette before too, but you obviously had no trouble in changing *that!*" His expression stiffened in self-reproach and Harriet realized that he regretted his reference to her changed appearance.

"Actually, it took a great deal of trouble. Don't you like my new look?"

"I hadn't considered it one way or the other," he said crushingly.

"Then my information was obviously at fault."

"What information?"

She couldn't back down now. "That you're allergic to blondes."

Retribution was as swift as it was shatteringly unexpected. "Only in bed."

SUSAN NAPIER was born on St. Valentine's Day, so it's not surprising she has developed an enduring love of romantic stories. She started her writing career as a journalist in Auckland, New Zealand, trying her hand at romantic fiction only after she had married her handsome boss! Numerous books later she still lives with her most enduring hero, two future heroes—her sons!—two cats and a computer. When she's not writing she likes to read and cook, often simultaneously!

Books by Susan Napier

HARLEQUIN PRESENTS
1554—SECRET ADMIRER
1595—WINTER OF DREAMS
1674—THE CRUELLEST LIE
1707—PHANTOM LOVER
1744—SAVAGE COURTSHIP
1788—THE SISTER SWAP

SUSAN NAPIER

Reckless Conduct

Harlequin Books

TORONTO • NEW YORK • LONDON
AMSTERDAM • PARIS • SYDNEY • HAMBURG
STOCKHOLM • ATHENS • TOKYO • MILAN
MADRID • WARSAW • BUDAPEST • AUCKLAND

ISBN 0-373-11847-3

RECKLESS CONDUCT

First North American Publication 1996.

CHAPTER ONE

MARCUS FOX slammed down the telephone and strode over to stand at the window of his nineteenth-floor office, glaring down at the sun-washed expanse of Aotea Square below.

The blunt fingers of one hand tapped on the barrel of an expensive telescope—the perfect executive toy for the perfect executive, his mother-in-law had teased him when she had given it to him at Christmas. Only to protect Susan's feelings from hurt had he permitted it to be set up in his office. Toys were for children. The last thing any executive of a large corporation needed was his work-space cluttered up with frivolous, time-wasting distractions.

He scowled.

A head-turning bottle-blonde in a miniskirt was sauntering diagonally across the square, creating a magnetic fluctuation in the wave of business-suited males fanning out from the pedestrian entrances to the underground car park. As if drawn by an invisible force, the men who were moving in the same direction automatically veered onto a close parallel path, while those who were approaching from another direction adjusted themselves on an intersecting line.

With an irritable grunt of self-derision he swivelled the telescope from its soothing view of the harbour and followed her progress across the square with a cynical, disapproving eye. He could tell that she was a bottle-blonde from the harsh reflection of the sun off the improbably white hair, and, from the length of leg she was

5

flashing and her provocative, hip-hitching walk, she was clearly revelling in the disruption that she was causing to the immediate male environment.

Marcus's mouth twisted contemptuously as one over-eager young voyeur ran into a rubbish bin while his head was screwed around trying to keep the legs in lustful sight for an extra few seconds. Silly idiot! Perhaps it would teach him a lesson, but somehow Marcus doubted it.

Thank God he was too old for such foolishness! He had finally conquered the dangerous fascination that sexy, artificial blondes had once held for his youthful self. Now he could look, and even admire, with a gratifying sense of detachment. Experience had taught him that women who paid most attention to outward artifice, those who presented the sexiest image, were usually the least exciting in bed and the most emotionally selfish. To Marcus, the brazen, feminine self-confidence being flaunted in the square presented not a provocative challenge to his masculinity but a tiresome reminder of his incipient problem.

An impatient shove sent the telescope tilting violently skywards on its axis.

Women!

At the moment he could cheerfully have consigned the whole sex to the very devil.

Except that he needed them . . . or, rather, he needed one special woman in particular.

And she, thank God, was the complete antithesis of the meretricious female parading her wares below!

CHAPTER TWO

'GOOD morning, Ted.'

Harriet nodded her usual pleasant greeting to the doughnut-munching security guard behind the main reception desk as she wafted past—although it was probably more of a wobble than a waft, she thought wryly, ignoring the strangled choking sound which was Ted's only response.

She wasn't used to the slender, four-inch heels that she was wearing. They clicked officiously against the polished marble floor of the lobby and had an unfortunate tendency to make her hips roll uncomfortably with every step. Walking was no longer the natural function she had always taken for granted and the narrowness of her short skirt further hampered her usually brisk stride.

She came to a stop by the bank of lifts, teetering unsteadily on her heels. As she reached for the button that would summon the express lift which serviced the upper floors a blunt masculine finger was there before her.

'Allow me.'

Harriet drew back, glancing sideways at the good-looking young man who had done a rapid shuffle up beside her.

'Why, thank you, Michael,' she murmured drily.

The trace of irony in her voice caused a flicker of puzzlement to dim the voltage of his confident smile slightly as she preceded him into the lift.

Michael Fleet was a stockbroker, known as 'the wolf of Finance Towers' by the females who worked in the twin buildings. Part of his infamous *modus operandi* was to use the notoriously slow lifts as a personal hunting ground in which to seek new prey. Harriet had witnessed his technique in action many times over the past six years but had never herself been deemed worthy of a second glance, let alone a smile.

Until today.

When Harriet turned she had a head-on view of Ted Sellers, his doughnut hanging limply from his stunned mouth, his bulging eyes rounded as he stared after her, the security of the building obviously the last thing on his mind. A surge of mischief made her lift her hand and waggle her fingers mockingly at him as the doors slid closed.

By the time Harriet tottered through the door to her office her good humour was flagging. Flirting up eighteen floors with Michael Fleet had been wickedly exhilarating, especially when he had belatedly realised who it was that he was trying to chat up. But when she'd departed from the lift the bright façade of cheerful insouciance that she had donned that morning with her new make-up and clothes had been sorely tested by the seething speculation that had stalked her through the sea of busy computer workstations in the main offices of Trident Finance.

Reaching the small suite of corner offices occupied by the accounts section, she felt as if she had just run a bruising gauntlet.

It was her own fault, of course. Usually she was one of the first to arrive at the office and was unobtrusively working at her desk when everyone else began to trickle in. Today she had been deliberately late. She had thought that a grand entrance would get all the fuss over and done with in one fell swoop. Now she wondered whether it wouldn't have been better to exercise a little caution and break her co-workers in gently to her flamboyant new image. She had had no idea that being interesting would be such hard work!

But no! She nipped that treacherous thought grimly in the bud. Caution was the watchword of the *old* Harriet Smith—the boring, pathetically conventional Harriet. The new, improved Harriet wasn't afraid of drawing attention to herself. She was assertive, self-confident, spontaneous—her actions governed by the impulses of the moment rather than by the constricting dread of what other people might think.

To that end Harriet directed a dazzling smile at the attractive young woman sitting at the smaller of the two desks in the elegantly furnished office.

'Good morning, Barbara,' she greeted her breezily.

'Miss Smith!'

Harriet closed the door behind her and strolled over to her desk.

'Is something wrong? Have I got a smudge on my nose?' she enquired, turning to meet her assistant's fascinated stare.

Barbara Martin almost swallowed her tongue in her hurry to back away from the direct challenge.

'Uh—n-no. Well, I mean—you're so, so...' She trailed off on seeing the militant gleam which sparked in Harriet's blue eyes, and hurriedly summoned the diplomacy expected of a budding executive secretary.

'That is, you're so *late*... I've been trying to ring you at home. Mr Jessop's been on hot bricks waiting for you to arrive. He's been buzzing for you every five minutes...'

Harriet bit her tongue to stop herself leaping to attention with a string of worried questions.

'Really?' she said carelessly, swinging the scarlet handbag that matched her shoes and jaunty silk jacket. She sat down in her swivel chair, opened her bag and took out a slim powder compact.

'In a bad mood, is he?' she murmured, opening the compact and dabbing at the non-existent shine on her nose.

It had taken her a good half-hour to put on her make-up this morning—something that normally took her ten minutes—and she was relieved to see that it still looked immaculate. She had followed the instructions in the personalised booklet that she had been given at the beauty salon to the letter and was gratified by the result.

Her deep-set eyes no longer seemed to recede into her face, and the fullness of her lips was accentuated with scarlet gloss rather than subdued with her usual dusky pink lipstick. Her thick, straight brows had been ruthlessly plucked into graceful arches and a contour blusher made the most of her pronounced cheek-bones.

Every woman was unique, the make-up artist at the salon had told her, and the trick was to play up that uniqueness rather than try to imitate the air-brushed perfection of models in glossy magazines. Harriet might never be able to lay claim to beauty but at least now nobody could call her inconspicuous!

Her flippant comment hung in the air, and in the oval compact mirror she could see the by now familiar glazed look creeping across Barbara Martin's face as she compared the frivolous Tuesday-morning version of Harriet Smith with the soberly dressed, quietly conventional woman she had last seen on the eve of the long weekend.

The former Miss Smith had always discouraged gossip and flippancy in the office, insisting on a businesslike formality at all times. It had been Harriet's serious demeanour and innate discretion combined with her excellent secretarial skills which had secured her early promotion to the position of personal secretary to Brian Jessop, head of Trident Finance's accounts section. She had only been twenty, but even then she had possessed an air of maturity and serene competence which had soon silenced the jealous criticism that an older, more experienced employee should have been given the job.

Now twenty-six, Harriet was ruefully aware that most people assumed that she was quite a bit older, mentally lumping her in with the rest of the executive secretaries at Trident, all of whom were well over thirty. Yet she did stand out from them in one respect—her patience and gentle personality made her a good trainer of junior staff. Harriet Smith was known to be strict but never temperamental or bitchy. Ambitious juniors like Barbara had taken to jostling for assignments to Brian Jessop's office, knowing that it would improve their own chances of promotion if it was noted on their personnel files that they had been groomed by the superbly efficient Miss Smith.

No wonder Barbara was looking as if she had just been hit in the face by a wet fish. She probably had hideous visions of her career crash-diving if her mentor's sanity was suddenly called into question.

'What? Oh! No. At least, I—I don't think so...' Barbara finally managed to summon the presence of mind to babble.

Harriet snapped the compact shut and grinned at her. 'Just another one of his pointless panics, then, is it?'

Unnerved by the friendly grin as much as the irreverent reference to their boss's sometimes volatile nature, Barbara smiled weakly back.

'I don't know... he said something about God not making things easy for him—I don't know whether he was being religious or profane.'

'Hmm, knowing Mr Jessop, it's bound to be profane,' said Harriet, lapsing into a tartly disapproving tone that made Barbara's smile blossom with relieved recognition.

'He has been swearing rather a lot,' she offered, glancing towards the closed door to the inner office. 'I had to make him three cups of coffee before he said it tasted right. But I always make the coffee that way. It was no different from the coffee he gets any other morning!'

'I'd better go in, then,' sighed Harriet, taking pity on her assistant's evident anxiety. Barbara had shaped up extremely well in the two months she had been with them, but she still lacked the self-confidence to handle an irate boss.

Well, might as well get it over with, she thought. Unconsciously squaring her padded shoulders, Harriet knocked briefly and marched into Brian Jessop's office without the customary pause for permission.

'You wanted to see me, Mr Jessop?'

She had been going to use his Christian name but at the last moment her nerve failed her, and she mentally cursed herself for her cowardice.

Brian Jessop was sitting at his desk in his shirtsleeves, just on the verge of taking a sip from his steaming cup. His blond head jerked at the sight of her and he inhaled sharply, sucking coffee into his air passages. He was immediately struck by a coughing fit, spewing coffee down his crisp white shirt-front and costly silk tie.

Harriet walked around the desk and thumped him heartily on the back, further slopping the coffee out of the cup and over his hand and shirt-cuff.

'Wha—? Miss Smith? Harriet! *Harry?*' he spluttered, the cup crashing back into its saucer as he lurched unsteadily to his feet. He swept a stylishly folded silk handkerchief out of his jacket pocket and began to blot distractedly at the mess on his shirt-front.

'Oh, my God, Harry, what's happened? What have you *done*?' His tone was one of utter consternation as he swept her a comprehensive look that took in the full impact of the red high heels, narrow black miniskirt, the filmy white blouse under the cropped red jacket and the slick make-up job.

'It's only coffee; it'll wash out,' she said soothingly, deliberately misunderstanding him.

'Not me! You! What in God's name has happened to your *hair*?' His normally low-pitched voice almost hit a screech as he stared, aghast, at the top of her head where she usually pinned her neat brown bun.

She lifted her chin high. 'I bleached it.'

Well, actually, *she* hadn't done the bleaching, the hairdresser had, and a very long and expensive process it had been too, when combined with a cut and blow-dry, a facial and manicure. But worth every cent, Harriet had decided faintly when the hairdresser had finally held up the mirror to show her the radical new image she had chosen for herself.

While she was growing up Harriet's mother had drummed it into her that a woman's hair *au naturel* was her crowning glory, and accordingly Harriet had always worn hers long and straight, pinning it tidily up when she was at work or leaving it in a thick plait.

Now it was a glaringly *un*natural platinum blonde that was, fortunately, flattering to her olive skin. It was also short and bouncy, the clever cut having revealed a natural wave that enabled her to sweep back the fringe in a careless, finger-tousled look.

'But why? Why *now*, of all times?' Brian Jessop groaned, scrubbing despairingly at his ruined shirt.

Harriet shrugged. She had no intention of going into the depressing details. The new Harriet was a woman without a past, a woman of the future!

'I felt like it.'

'You *felt* like it?' he howled, and Harriet frowned, disappointed by the strength of his negative reaction. She had expected her boss to be startled, yes—amused even, but hardly horrified. After all, he was married to a glamorous model who changed her hair colour at the drop of a hat.

'I don't believe it. A damned *blonde*...in a peek-a-boo blouse no less.' He shook his head violently. 'You can't *do* this to me, Harry.'

Harriet began to get irritated. 'I haven't done anything to *you*,' she pointed out with a tinge of sarcasm. 'And this blouse has two layers of chiffon. It's opaque, not peek-a-boo.'

He ignored her disgruntled protest, his eyes dropping to her hemline. To her amazement he actually flushed.

'And, my God, look at your *legs*!'

He pointed accusingly.

Harriet obediently looked down at her lacy black stockings. 'What's the matter with them?' Like the rest of Harriet her legs were a little on the thin side, but fairly ordinary as far as she could judge.

'There's far too much of them showing, that's what!' he growled.

This from a man whose wife frolicked in a basque across city billboards promoting a famous line of sexy lingerie! Harriet repressed an incredulous laugh.

'Lots of women are wearing miniskirts again,' she said patiently. 'It's the fashion.'

'But not *your* fashion,' he insisted with fervent persuasion. 'You're always so modest and discreet; classic clothes for the office environment—isn't that what you call them? For goodness' sake, in all the years you've worked for me you've never even displayed a *knee*!' He sounded outraged at the very thought.

'Well, now you know that I have two of them like everyone else,' said Harriet crisply. So she used to be as stodgy and bland as rice pudding—from now on he would just have to get used to soufflé!

Brian Jessop ran a hand through his thick golden hair, his tanned face creasing into anxious lines as he announced, 'You'll just have to go home and change, that's all. As quick as you can. Take a taxi—charge it to the firm. And for goodness' sake wash that stuff out of your hair!'

Now it was Harriet's turn to be outraged. 'I can't wash it out; it's bleach.'

If the first consequence of her being a new woman was to be fired for insubordination, then so be it.

'Then dye it back!' he ordered.

'Back to mousy brown?' She looked at him incredulously. 'Why ever would I want to do that?'

'Because *I* ask you to. Would you? *Please*, Harry; you don't—'

The telephone on his desk burred softly, interrupting his pleading, and he snatched it up, inadvertently hitting the speaker button as he fumbled the handpiece from the cradle to his ear.

'*What?*'

There was a brief silence in response to his snarling demand and then a familiar voice, carrying a faint tinge of dry amusement, rang out from the speaker.

'You sound harassed, Brian. Don't tell me your little paragon hasn't turned up yet. And here I thought she was infallible—'

Harriet looked sharply at her boss as he quickly punched off the speaker, cutting off the rest of the comment.

'*No!* No...er...no, as a matter of fact she hasn't—' His normally frank brown eyes were suddenly furtive as he half turned his back on Harriet's curious gaze and dropped his voice.

'That is, she won't be coming in today—as a matter of fact she just called in sick... Quite ill apparently... Uh—no, she isn't, not very often...'

Harriet's suspicions strengthened and she leaned around his blocking shoulder to demand in soft, clear tones, 'Are you talking about me?'

Brian Jessop clapped his large hand urgently over the receiver and hissed at her to be quiet.

'No, no idea, I'm afraid,' he continued heartily to his unseen caller, 'but if I hear anything else I'll let you know. Perhaps someone else could—? Oh, yes, quite... quite. Oh, dear... well, perhaps Personnel can help you out in the meantime. Yes, yes, of course I will...'

He muttered a few more comments with a strained combination of deference and barely concealed impatience before hurriedly hanging up.

'You were talking about me, weren't you?' Harriet demanded immediately.

'Hmm?' He escaped around the other side of his desk and began to poke vaguely about in the pile of correspondence on his blotter.

Be assertive, Harriet reminded herself. Stand up for yourself. Don't be a doormat. Act *blonde*.

'Mr Jessop? *Brian!*' Her unprecedented informality succeeded where politeness had failed. He looked shocked but attentive as she challenged, 'That was Mr Fox on the phone; I recognised his voice.'

It was impossible to mistake the distinctive cool drawl of the chairman of the board of Trident Finance. Marcus Fox had inherited the insurance company on the death of his father-in-law a decade previously, but although Gerald Jerome might have founded the business it had been his shrewd young son-in-law who, with characteristic forethought and caution, had taken the company public and expanded and diversified its financial interests to create a new, blue-chip investment stock. The Fox name was synonymous with trustworthiness and solidarity and he commanded an immense respect from his employees—Harriet included.

'It *was* Mr Fox, wasn't it?' she persisted.

Cornered, her boss nodded reluctantly. 'Well, yes, actually it was.' He rustled the papers hopefully on his desk. 'Oh, dear, I was sure the Cartwright folio was here somewhere; would you mind checking the files for me?'

Harriet's blue eyes narrowed at this blatant attempt at evasion. The old Harriet would have retreated and meekly done as she was bid, willing to accept the hint that it was none of her business.

'After you've answered my question. Who was the "little paragon" Mr Fox was referring to—the one you said had called in sick?'

There wasn't much doubt in her mind. She knew that her boss liked to boast about his 'perfect' secretary. She should have been flattered that the chairman claimed to believe her a model of excellence, but this morning the prissiness of the label annoyed her. Paragons had no character. She didn't want to be some unflawed piece of boring office furniture; she wanted to be alive and vital and gloriously, fallibly human. And being called 'little' diminished her sense of self-importance even further. Five feet five wasn't *little*, she thought aggressively; it was *average*.

Her boss cleared his throat authoritatively. 'Look, Harry, we have a great deal to get through this morning. You being late has thrown everything out of kilter—'

Harriet snorted. She was not going to be deflected from her purpose by misplaced guilt.

'My proper name is Harriet; please use it,' she said, suddenly realising how much the masculine contraction of her name grated. Brian Jessop had coined it soon after she'd come to work for him—although in deference to her dignity he only used it when they were alone—and she had been too polite to protest. Now, however, it was wildly inappropriate to her new, sexy self-image. 'If you won't tell me what that call was about,

I suppose I'll just have to ring Miss Broadbent and ask if she knows,' she continued calmly.

Very much a working chairman, Mr Fox had a penthouse office suite which was the hub of his business empire. When he travelled, which was a great deal, he was accompanied by a personal staff of three, but he also maintained a full quota of office staff and when he was in residence he worked extremely long hours. Harriet had been co-opted numerous times to help ease the workload on Clare Broadbent, his home-office secretary. She was an iron-haired, iron-plated lady approaching her retirement years, something of an institution at Trident, having worked for Gerald Jerome up until his death. Harriet got on extremely well with her, to the extent that it had been hinted that if she didn't blot her copybook Clare might consider recommending her as a suitable successor.

A muscle began to twitch in Brian Jessop's cheek as he recognised the subtle threat. 'Now, Harry—er—Harriet, don't overreact...'

She looked him straight in the eye. 'I'm not the one overreacting. That call was about me, wasn't it? And you lied. You actually lied to the chairman of the board!'

Impaled on her accusing stare, Brian Jessop winced, rallied and began to bluster. 'What else could I do? He rang down first thing this morning and asked if he could borrow you for some urgent personal project. Wanted to know if I could manage with just Barbara and a junior for a few weeks. Of course I said yes... I didn't know you were going to walk in this morning looking like...like—' He foundered, momentarily lost for words.

'What has the way I look got to do with anything?' Harriet demanded haughtily.

'Dammit, it has everything to do with it.' He began to pace up and down behind his desk. 'You know how punctilious Marcus is, what a stickler he is for doing things properly. For goodness' sake, he's even more conservative than you are...were...*are*!' The re-correction was forcefully stressed.

'Why do you think you're his first choice whenever he needs an extra secretary? I'll tell you why: because he knows you're going to slot in with his team without being obstructive or distracting.' He continued ticking her assets off on his fingers. 'You're loyal, punctual, polite and conscientious. You never panic in a crisis or quibble about doing overtime or whine for appreciation for simply doing what you're paid to do.'

Harriet scowled. His paean of supposed flattery confirmed her worst suspicions about herself. Had she really been that nondescript, self-effacing and submissive? That much of a goody-two-shoes?

Yes! came the resounding answer from the depths of her being.

And look at where it had got her—in a rut so deep that the walls had begun collapsing in on her, threatening to smother her alive. In the past year she had suffered blow after blow and doggedly soldiered on, fending off the pain by keeping herself busy, relying increasingly on her work to provide her with a sense of stability amid the catastrophic upheavals in her private life.

Latterly, though, even that source of security had been threatened as Harriet had begun to wake each morning with a crippling sense of dread, a deep reluctance to get out of bed and face the new day.

Friday evening had changed all that. The last, shattering blow had jolted Harriet out of her state of drifting depression into one of pure rage. The cleansing anger had swept away the enervating sense of helplessness which had pervaded her being for the past few months. She was tired of being a victim of capricious fate. From now on she was going to stop worrying about what the future might hold and concentrate on enjoying the pleasures of the moment.

Ever since she had made the momentous decision to change her life she had shimmered with fierce energy. She had wrenched herself back into the sunlight through sheer force of will and she had no intention of letting herself sink back into that ditch of melancholy stagnation. *Ever.*

'What are you going to say when Mr Fox discovers I'm not off sick at all?' she probed. 'You can't expect him not to find out I'm still around the office.'

Brian Jessop rubbed his jaw anxiously. 'Yes, but by then maybe you'll be back to normal...'

His suggestion that the radical change in her appearance was just some temporary aberration on her part was infuriating, if understandable. No doubt he expected Harriet to come to her senses and revert to the boring, mousy creature whose most admired qualities were her loyalty and uncomplaining devotion to duty. Only time would prove him wrong.

Harriet tossed her head defiantly, revelling in the soft flurry of hair which caressed her cheeks. She looked good, she felt good and nobody was going to be permitted to undermine her intention to live life rather than merely endure it!

'This *is* normal, Brian. This is *me*, the way that I am. Mr Fox may as well get used to it now as later. So why don't I just go on up and see what he wants?'

Brian Jessop looked alarmed. 'God, no; just stay out of the way and let me think of the best way to handle it,' he said hurriedly, his frustration getting the better of him as he added, 'Why in the hell couldn't you have decided to be a redhead? I happen to know that Marcus has an extreme aversion to blonde bimbos; the last thing he's going to want is one swanning around his executive suite—'

'*Blonde bimbos!*' Harriet flushed with angry mortification. She had been very careful not to go overboard and turn herself into the caricature of a woman. She wanted to be *looked* at, not laughed at, and her instinctive good taste had prevented her desire for flash-and-dash from getting out of hand. Hadn't it? She felt her confidence waver and fiercely attacked to defend it.

'Are you telling me that just because I change the colour of my hair and wear more trendy clothes my employer is entitled to assume I've suddenly become brainless as well?' she demanded. 'Because if that's what you're saying it's the grossest piece of discrimination I've ever encountered!' Her blue eyes glowed with contempt for his reasoning as she added with repressive certainty, 'Anyway, you can't tell me that Mr Fox would use a cheap, derogatory word like "bimbo" to describe a woman. He's too much of a gentleman...'

A gleam of humour leavened the worry in Brian Jessop's brown eyes at this naïve expression of faith. 'I assure you it's exactly the word he would use. Believe me, when men talk to other men over a few drinks they frequently use words they edit out when they talk to women. Even gentlemen...perhaps most *especially* gentlemen... Let's just say that to date Marcus has been negatively impressed by the fair-haired women in his life.'

Harriet's blue eyes regarded him stonily and he sighed.

'Look—he mentioned that this project is personal and rather delicate, right? That was the exact word he used—*delicate*—so I think we can safely interpret him to mean *low-profile*. He wants someone who won't draw undue attention to what's going on. Forgive me, Harry—et, but at the moment there's no way you're going to be able to work around here without attracting a good deal of attention!'

From her experiences already that morning Harriet knew him to be right but she was not in a mood to be sweet and co-operative. 'Only for a few days. Once everyone gets over the shock they'll find someone else to gossip about—'

'Don't you believe it. It's certainly going to take *me* more than a few days. I liked you the way you were,' he tacked on with the disgruntled air of a sulky boy.

Yes, because you could walk all over me without any hint of opposition, thought Harriet, but she said calmly, 'Well, *I* didn't. And talking of the importance of appearances—don't you think you'd better freshen up before your first appointment?'

'Oh, hell, is that the time?' He looked down at his watch, and was freshly aghast at the patchy brown stains blotching his shirt-front. 'I suppose I'm going to have to—'

Harriet had already whipped an almost identical white shirt, beautifully pressed, from the closet by the door. She handed it to him wordlessly, along with a fresh tie.

He gave her a winning smile as he took them. 'Thanks, Harry; you always come up trumps in a tight corner.'

'Harriet,' she corrected, smiling back at him. He needn't think that he could manipulate her with his approval. She was no longer a pathetic creature who depended on others to validate her actions. She was a free-thinking and free-spirited woman.

'Oh, right . . . Harriet.' Like Barbara, he was unnerved by the suggestion of mischief in her face and the dimple that suddenly flirted in her cheek. Since when had his prim Miss Smith had dimples?

It was an indication of Brian Jessop's distraction that he stripped off his shirt and tie on the spot rather than retreating to the small bathroom attached to the office. He swore as he discovered that he'd forgotten to undo his cuff-links, struggling for a moment in the entangling sleeves, managing to extricate one hand before being defeated by his own impatience.

'You're going to tear it if you carry on like that. Here, let me,' Harriet offered boldly. A small, neat hand steadied his wrist as her slender fingers laboriously picked at the tiny piece of material that had somehow become wedged into the hinge of the cuff-link. Thank goodness for the miracle of fake fingernails, she thought wryly as she wielded her red-painted talons like tweezers. She only hoped that she would still be able to type as easily with her extended digits!

'You're always so willing to pitch in when you're needed, Harriet,' he said encouragingly to her bent head. 'That's another reason you rank so high in Marcus's approval.'

Translation: you're incapable of saying no.

'*No*, Brian, I'm *not* going home to change,' she took pleasure in firmly stating. 'Nor am I going to skulk around here as if I'm guilty of a crime. The only way you're going to get me to leave is to fire me. In which case I shall sue you for wrongful dismissal.'

'What ever happened to your famous rule about respect for authority?' he grouched. 'Shouldn't you be calling me Mr Jessop and briskly obeying my every command...?'

'Somehow you don't seem so very authoritative now I've seen you half-naked,' she replied, flicking him a pert look. To her surprise and amusement her sophisticated boss flushed and squirmed in discomfort.

'Good God, Harriet, don't say things like that. People might get the wrong idea...'

'Stop panicking,' she dared to tease as she finally worked the recalcitrant cuff-link free and watched him hurriedly shoulder himself into his clean shirt. 'You're letting your imagination run away with you. I'm sure Mr Fox isn't as easily shockable as you seem to think. Being a rampant perfectionist doesn't make him a perfect human being himself, you know—more likely the exact opposite. He's probably riddled with insecurities behind that poker-face. He's more likely to go off the deep end at the idea of being deceived than he is at some minor infringement of office etiquette—'

'A point of view with which I thoroughly concur.'

The silky-smooth observation made them both jump. They spun around to stare in dismay at the door which had opened soundlessly behind them.

Marcus Fox stood squarely in the doorway, one hand thrust casually into his pocket, his cool blue eyes studying Brian Jessop's frantic attempts to button his gaping shirt and simultaneously thrust the crisp white tails into the top of his trousers.

Harriet's bold confidence wavered. She had a sinking feeling that her fabulous plan to revolutionise herself was just about to receive its first set-back.

CHAPTER THREE

'I APOLOGISE for eavesdropping,' said Marcus Fox in a singularly unapologetic tone. 'You were both so absorbed in your... *discussion* that you obviously didn't hear me knock.'

The subtle emphasis was accompanied by an interrogative lift of thick black brows, which nearly caused Brian Jessop to strangle himself as he stepped forward, urgently knotting his tie on top of his unbuttoned collar.

Harriet knew that look well. It was capable of making even the purest of innocents feel mired in guilt. She struggled to control her instinctive blush, grateful that her boss's anxious movement had blocked her off from the laser-like blue gaze. She mentally made herself as small as she could behind his back.

One brief glimpse of Mr Fox's expression had been enough to justify her unease. He had looked entirely too self-satisfied for a man supposedly confronting the unexpected. If they hadn't heard him knock it was because he *hadn't* knocked. He had fully intended to barge in on whatever was happening inside Brian's office. Something in the telephone conversation had alerted his curiosity and with his customary decisiveness he had shot down to investigate.

'Uh—Marcus—good heavens! I—we—this isn't what you might think...' Brian Jessop's rushed protest died, sounding like the perfect cliché of guilt, even to Harriet's sympathetic ears.

She didn't blame him for feeling flustered. Marcus Fox's appearance often had the effect of making people feel at a disadvantage. He was only a shade over six feet in height but to Harriet he had always seemed overwhelmingly large. Perhaps it was the breadth of his shoulders and the evident toughness of the lean-hipped, long-legged body, but more likely it was his sheer personal presence. Where other men relied on words or macho theatrics to dominate, Marcus Fox could effectively control a meeting with his silences.

And yet his toughness was to a certain extent an illusion. His stern face with its bold nose, square mouth and determined chin, and the perpetual threatening frown created by thick, straight brows over hooded eyes, presented an image that was forbiddingly harsh, but over the years Harriet had decided that Mr Fox was one of the most subtly refined men that she had ever encountered. 'One of nature's gentlemen', as Clare Broadbent was wont to boast discreetly.

Like his hair, raven-black and close-cut, he was intensely physically controlled. He never lost his temper or his cool, and was courteous to his staff even when he was chewing them out. His unyielding sense of honour was legendary in an intensely competitive business environment where personal ethics were often considered as negotiable as bearer bonds.

Brian Jessop cleared his throat and tried again. 'I...er...spilled my coffee, you see, and we were just changing my shirt—'

'*We?*' The deep, resonant voice was mocking. 'Do you mean to tell me that one of my most senior executives has yet to learn how to dress himself?'

Harriet mistrusted the hint of sardonic amusement. The stern chairman of Trident wasn't renowned for his sense of humour. She was suddenly impatient with her boss for his floundering, and with herself for trying to fade into the background. She was falling back into old bad habits already!

She boldly stepped out into the open. 'Mr Jessop's cuff-link got caught and since it was my fault he spilled his coffee I felt it was the least I could do to help untangle him.'

'You know what a whiz Miss Smith is at untangling knotty problems,' Brian Jessop joked weakly.

'Miss Smith?' Marcus Fox's head turned sharply, all his concentration abruptly shifting onto Harriet. As his ice-blue gaze swept her a lightning glance from head to foot his pupils seem to shrink into tiny black pinpoints, but when he blinked an instant later they were normal size again and Harriet decided that she must have imagined that fleeting visual recoil.

Not a muscle had altered in his expression as his eyes returned to hers.

'Ah...yes, Miss Smith,' he murmured blandly. 'You've had a miraculous recovery, I take it?'

She didn't pretend to misunderstand him. It was obvious that he must have identified her voice in the background during the telephone call.

'I wasn't ill, sir,' she said flatly, piqued by his lack of reaction to the Harriet Mark 2 model. So much for Brian Jessop's fear of lobbing a blonde bombshell into the chairman's face; she had fizzled like a damp squib. The man was impervious to shock—it would probably take a nuclear explosion to buckle that iron dignity.

'No? That's not what Brian led me to understand.'

Aware of her boss's strangled apprehension, Harriet took another reckless step into the unknown. She brazenly lied, 'Mr Jessop was rather confused himself. When I rang early this morning to let him know I'd be late for work, and to remind him of several things that required his serious attention, the messages unfortunately got mixed up—'

'Who?'

She was disconcerted by the interruption to her inventive flow.

'I beg your pardon?'

'Who was it who took the message?'

'Oh.' She saw the danger immediately. She couldn't allow some poor, innocent switchboard operator to take the heat for her outrageous lie. 'It wasn't a *who*, it was a *what*. The answering machine was playing up, and when Mr Jessop tried to replay the garbled messages for clarification they were completely wiped off.'

Pleased at her cleverness in tying up all possible loose ends, Harriet tried out the glitzy smile that she had practised in the mirror all weekend. She tossed back her startlingly pale hair and smoothed her palms down the side-seams of her miniskirt. To her frustration the hooded blue gaze didn't waver from hers.

'Have you reported the fault to the telephone company?' he enquired mildly.

And to think she used to admire him for his meticulous attention to petty details! She shrugged—a gesture of subtle insolence which would have horrified her a week ago. It felt good. 'I haven't had the chance yet.'

'I see...'

She feared that he did, but she also knew that he couldn't prove a thing. She hung onto her smile and batted her baby-blues innocently, making the most of her lavishly mascaraed eyelashes.

Brian Jessop cleared his throat again and readjusted his tie with evident relief. 'Yes...it was all a bit confusing, but we've cleared it up now. Uh...I was just explaining to Miss Smith about your phone call—'

'So I inferred...'

His dry comment prompted a tiny silence as they all remembered the conversation from which he had drawn that inference. Exactly how much had he overheard?

Harriet wondered, and then decided defiantly that she didn't care.

'Since I'm here I can save you any more unnecessary explanations, Brian,' he continued in the same ambiguous tone. 'No doubt you'll want to get busy with your own work so Miss Smith will accompany me back to my office and I can brief her there.'

'Oh, but—'

The beetling black brows rose ominously. 'You have a problem with that, Brian?' The hard mouth crimped at one corner when no immediate answer was forthcoming.

'No? Good; that's settled, then. Miss Smith?' He turned sideways and extended his arm towards the door, inviting her to precede him. No, *commanding* . . .

Correctly interpreting her boss's rolling eyes, Harriet folded her hands meekly in front of her and stonewalled in her best secretary-speak. 'Yes, of course, Mr Fox. But there are one or two essentials I need to organise with Mr Jessop if I'm going to be away, so perhaps I could follow you up in a few minutes . . . ?'

'I'm afraid not.' He denied her request smoothly. 'I have a meeting shortly which is going to require my full attention and I need to have this thing settled before I go in. You can resume your cosy little tête-à-tête with Brian later.'

It was evident that he had no intention of allowing them to confer alone and, with a helpless glance at Brian Jessop's resigned face, Harriet reluctantly allowed herself to be shepherded through to the outer office.

She paused beside her desk to pick up her handbag and listened sourly to Marcus Fox charm a flustered Barbara with the grave assurance that he was sure she'd cope superbly in her senior's absence.

Then followed the embarrassment of being marched back through the main office at a speed that threatened to have her falling flat on her face. What price her image of slinky sophistication now? Harriet felt like a naughty schoolgirl being dragged off to detention by a stern-faced headmaster in front of the whole school. Not that she knew what that felt like—in school she had never done anything to merit public chastisement.

A wobbly red heel twisted and Harriet stumbled and was brought up by a large hand shooting out to cup her elbow. It remained there, hard and disconcertingly warm through the thin silk of her jacket, distracting her from the hush of astonishment that marked their brisk passage across the room.

Oh, well, this was what she had wanted, wasn't it? Drama? Excitement? New experiences with which to colour the depressingly blank canvas of her life? Perhaps this special project of Mr Fox's would be something that she could fling herself into with wild enthusiasm, a chance to extend herself professionally, to discover the true extent of her unrealised potential.

As they reached the lift the doors opened and Michael Fleet sauntered out, reading a sheaf of computer printouts. He grinned when he saw Harriet.

'Hey, babe, long time no see.' He winked as he strolled past them, then turned to walk backwards down the hall as he continued brashly, 'Listen, about that date we made earlier... I just found out I have an appointment this evening. How about if I pick you up an hour later and we leave dinner until after the show? Then I thought we could go on to Lizzie's.'

'Oh, y-yes, sure... fine,' was all Harriet had a chance to stammer as she was steered forcefully into the lift. For one cowardly moment she had been relieved by the thought that Michael had changed his mind and was trying to cry off. Instead he was going to extend their evening by taking her to the city's hottest new nightclub.

'Great. See you at seven-thirty, then...'

As the doors began to close, the bone-tingling grip dropped away from her elbow. Harriet knew that Marcus Fox was staring at her profile but she resolutely refused to look at him.

Babe?

Michael thought she was a *babe*? She tried to feel flattered but she suspected that a babe was no classier than a bimbo. Or maybe he had called her that because he had forgotten her Christian name. Given the number of women he dated it was quite likely!

'You're going out with Michael Fleet?'

The enquiry seemed perfectly polite but the hint of incredulity in the deep voice made Harriet stiffen.

'Yes.'

'Have you dated before?' He pressed the button for the top floor.

Primed for an insult by the rage that simmered just below the surface of her bright, new façade, Harriet jerked her chin around to glare at him.

'Of course I've dated. I'm perfectly normal in that respect,' she exploded. 'I've gone out with lots of men. Did you think I used to sit at home every night doing my knitting?' It had been reading rather than knitting, but, still, her words held the power of literal truth.

There was a small pause.

'I meant have you been on a date with *Michael* before,' he said gently.

'Oh!' Harriet blushed with mortification, aware of how telling her defensive outburst must have been to his shrewd intelligence. 'No,' she admitted in a small, stifled voice.

'And he asked you out for the first time...this morning?' he probed delicately.

It was none of his business and Harriet longed to tell him so, but she had already made enough of a fool of herself by overreacting to an innocuous question.

'Yes. In the lift, on my way up to work.' The gratuitous information quivered with defiance.

'I see.'

No, he didn't, Harriet thought resentfully. How could he? He didn't know what was going on inside her. She watched his big body shift, as if accepting an invisible burden, his shoulders flexing as he flicked open the jacket of his elegant suit and thrust his hand into his trouser pocket. She nibbled her lip nervously as it struck her that his casual stance was out of character for a man whose body language was usually as formal and unrevealing as his attire.

Marcus Fox was an orderly man, too self-controlled ever to fidget or slouch around with his hands in his pockets. In the business arena he wore his identically tailored dark suits and white shirts like armour, and wielded his cool detachment like a weapon. He didn't engage in the kind of idle personal chit-chat that he was indulging in now, not without a precise purpose, anyhow. He wasn't prone to impulse. When presented with a problem he carefully pondered all sides before taking action, and once he had exercised his cautious judgement he never deviated from his decision.

At the moment he was regarding Harriet with a brooding look of frustration which suggested that she was a particularly knotty problem.

'Fleet has quite a reputation in the building.'

She had learned her lesson about jumping to conclusions and endeavoured to respond pleasantly, 'Yes, I know. They say he has clients clamouring for him to manage their portfolios—'

'I was talking about his reputation with *women*,' he said heavily.

'Oh!'

'It's not very good, I'm afraid.'

She was unable to prevent a smile of satisfaction. 'So I've heard.'

Her cheerful reply earned her a reproving frown. 'Then you probably know that he's not interested in steady relationships or emotional involvement. To put it bluntly, he's a master of the one-night stand. Once he's achieved his aim he moves on. He's addicted to the thrill of the chase and he considers any woman who accepts a date with him as fair game.'

'Really...' Harriet gritted her teeth at his patronising tone. She knew that Marcus Fox had a highly developed sense of responsibility towards his employees, but until now she had never considered him pompous. Not only had he insulted her by totally ignoring her sparkling new image, but, like Brian Jessop, he evidently thought that the changes were purely cosmetic. He was telling her that staid, unadventurous Harriet Smith couldn't possibly cope with the attentions of sophisticated, fun-loving Michael Fleet.

The lift came to a halt and she watched in angry disbelief as Marcus Fox placed his large hand over the control panel to delay the door opening so that he could continue his infuriating little homily.

'Not only is Fleet indiscriminate, but he has no respect for the woman's privacy when he notches up a victory. He's an inveterate boaster about his conquests. He's even been known to bet on the outcome of a date. All he's interested in is having a good time, and he expects the women he goes out with to have the same free-and-easy morals—'

'Good!' she snapped, using the element of surprise to grasp his solid wrist and push it sharply away from the control buttons so that the doors sprang open.

'Good?' Marcus Fox stayed rooted to the spot as she stepped out onto the thick grey carpet of the executive-suite foyer. 'What do you mean—*good*?'

Harriet turned to look at him and was deeply gratified by his censorious expression. At last she had surprised a genuine reaction out of him!

'I mean good, he sounds like a really hot date,' she said with a reckless toss of her head.

'A hot date?' He repeated the words slowly, as if they were in an alien tongue.

'Yeah, you know—one where there's a lot of action.'

'Action?' The doors were closing on him and he darted out between them with a startling burst of agility for such a powerfully built man.

'Fun.'

His black brows lowered even further as he towered over her. 'You're going out with Michael Fleet for *fun*?' he rumbled.

'Well, I'm certainly not going out with him in order to have a perfectly miserable time,' she said sweetly.

He dismissed her dripping sarcasm with an impatient wave. 'Miss Smith, I wonder if you've quite grasped the import of my remarks?'

'Of course I have,' she said in exasperation. 'You're warning me that by tomorrow I'll just be another notch on the matchwood that passes for Michael's bedpost.'

'Miss Smith!'

'Mr Fox!'

It finally seemed to sink in that the paragon of secretarial virtues was thumbing her nose at her great leader's words of worldly wisdom. He muttered something harsh under his breath and forgot his gentlemanly manners sufficiently to turn on his heel and stride ahead of her through the open glass doors to their left. He paused briefly beside a grey-haired woman who was quietly tapping at her computer.

'No interruptions, please, Miss Broadbent. Miss Smith and I need to discuss her new duties.'

'Yes, Mr Fox.'

Harriet smiled weakly at Clare Broadbent as she stepped into the lady's sight-line. She had regretfully accepted that her new image would probably cause her to plummet dramatically in the older woman's estimation, but to her surprise she wasn't nailed with a look of frigid contempt. In fact as she walked jerkily into Marcus Fox's office in his impatient wake she could have sworn that she saw a twinkle of amusement eclipse the surprise in the faded brown eyes.

The inner office was as cool and dignified as the man who inhabited it, decorated in soothing shades of blue and grey and unadorned by any hint of frivolity. The large window was tinted, screening out most of the summer sun's damaging rays. Apart from a single, sombre portrait of Gerald Jerome behind the desk there were no paintings on the plain-papered walls or striking touches of personality in the furnishings. The huge desk dominated the room and the grey leather chairs and couch arranged around it were as functional as they were luxurious.

Harriet shook off the strange feeling of anxiety that gripped her as she looked at the furniture. There was no reason for her to feel uncomfortable. Everything was neat and in its rightful place.

The only thing that was unusual was the powerful, complicated-looking telescope squatting by the large window. Harriet remembered seeing it the last time she had been in the office nearly three months ago, but at the time she had been too puzzled by the chairman's behaviour to pay much attention to it. He had been vague and imprecise as to his reason for summoning her, and Harriet had been increasingly edgy herself until it had dawned on her that he must be trying to apologise delicately for the unfortunate events of New Year's Eve, a couple of nights previously. He had probably spoken

privately to each and every employee who had attended
the annual office party.

Because of the cultural and religious diversity of
Trident's workforce, the traditional Christmas do had
been eschewed in favour of a more neutral mark of appreciation for the year's work, but on this occasion the
delicious fruit punch which was offered along with beer
and wine had been liberally spiked by an employee who
had arrived already drunk. Some dangerous high jinks
and appallingly offensive behaviour had occurred as a
result, and Harriet had been grateful that her own un-
accustomed consumption had merely resulted in her
being wretchedly ill.

Marcus Fox had fired the man who had doctored the
punch, but Harriet considered it typical of his code of
ethics that he'd accepted personal responsibility as head
of the firm for the safety and welfare of his employees.

Only by strenuously assuring him that she had been
far too unwell to notice or care what was going on around
her had she succeeded in fending off his unshakeable
conviction that she must have been deeply embarrassed
by what had occurred. He had been so obviously ill at
ease with her calm rejection of his apologetic concern
that she had been glad to escape back to Brian Jessop,
who had treated the whole thing as a joke, albeit one in
very poor taste.

He wasn't ill at ease now, thought Harriet as she
watched Marcus Fox stride around his desk and past the
telescope to sink heavily into his leather swivel chair. He
leaned his elbows on the desk, steepling his fingers in
front of his mouth, and gave her his famous black-
browed look, every bit the imperious employer.

Harriet guessed that she was meant to quail. Her toes
curled in her shoes as she attempted to show that she
wasn't oppressed by his intimidating silence.

'Is astronomy one of your hobbies?'

'No.' The clipped monosyllable sternly discouraged her interest.

Quite. She didn't imagine that he had any hobbies. From what she had heard, he worked practically non-stop. Even at that notorious New Year's Eve party he had made only a fleeting appearance. A teetotaller, he had toasted the staff with the spiked punch and mingled sociably for a while, but, having just walked off a plane from London, he had been pale with fatigue, and Harriet had heard that he had disappeared long before the alcohol-fuelled mayhem had begun. She tried to imagine Marcus Fox letting his hair down and couldn't. He was always so serious, so controlled. He would never do anything reckless.

'What's the telescope for, then? Spying on the offices across the square?' she teased impulsively. 'Or do you use it for girl-watching?'

She couldn't quite believe that the brazen words had popped out of her own mouth, and he seemed similarly stunned. His jaw clenched and an unusual flush mounted the broad cheek-bones. His pale eyes glittered under lowered lids. This time his inspection of her was slow and nerve-rackingly thorough and Harriet's knees turned to jelly. He was trying to make her horribly self-conscious and he was succeeding, but at least he was finally deigning to acknowledge that the Harriet Smith he was dealing with was most definitely *not* the woman that he had previously taken so arrogantly for granted.

'Sit down, Miss Smith.'

It was an order, not an invitation. Harriet walked carefully over to the chair furthest from the desk, aware that the temporary weakness in her knees made her hips sway more than ever. However did models manage to slink down runways on their uncomfortable, high-fashion stilts? She thought wistfully of the comfortable, old-

fashioned court shoes that she had donated to the
Salvation Army, along with the rest of her old wardrobe.

She sat down with relief, only to find that her narrow
skirt shrank alarmingly up her slender thighs. She pretended not to notice. She hadn't taken into account things
like bending and twisting and sitting when she had been
burning up the boutiques during the long weekend. She
had just stood in front of the mirror and ruthlessly
bought whatever the shop assistant had recommended.

Harriet folded her hands in her diminished lap and
tried to remember everything she had ever read about
miniskirt etiquette. Did one cross one's legs or slant them
primly parallel to the side? The idea of being prim decided her. She slid one knee rashly over the top of the
other. The skirt retreated another crucial few centimetres.

Marcus Fox's steepled fingers collapsed and his voice
was slightly hoarse as he began ominously, 'Miss Smith,
I am about to break one of my cardinal rules about not
allowing personal problems to intrude on matters of
business.'

Harriet's jaw jutted sullenly. If he made one single
slighting comment *now* about her appearance, she would
throw it right back in his pompous face!

'Miss Smith, I have a daughter...'

Harriet stared at him blankly, wondering whether she
had misheard. 'A daughter?'

'Yes. Her name is Nicola. She's just turned fifteen.
A very mature fifteen, I might add,' he added wryly.

Harriet was bewildered. What did his daughter have
to do with *her*? Unless he was going to wrap up some
more of his unwelcome advice under the guise of talking
about his daughter's adolescent problems.

Yes, that must be it. Harriet's blue eyes darkened in
pain. He wasn't her father! Her father had been a wonderful man and not at all like Marcus Fox. He was gone

now, like her mother and her harum-scarum older brother, Tim. Like Keith. Like Frank—

Her mind slammed shut on the grim litany. She wasn't going to dwell on it. She was tough, a survivor, not some feeble-willed green girl who believed in stardust and fairy tales. She knew exactly where she was going with her life and why. She certainly didn't need Marcus Fox's paternalistic concern. The only person she had to please these days was *herself* . . .

'Miss Smith, are you listening to me?'

The deeply nettled tone finally penetrated Harriet's abstraction and she tried to look alert and interested.

'I'm sorry?'

'I'm *trying* to tell you about my daughter.' His strained patience warned her not to push him too far.

'I didn't know you had any children,' she said, reluctant to give him any encouragement for the lecture that she was certain was in store.

Marcus Fox was known to defend his privacy rigorously. In spite of his position and wealth he lived a very low-profile life, which meant that he was rarely the subject of speculation, either for his staff or the Press. Harriet knew only the bare bones—that he had a house in the country and a serviced apartment somewhere in the city, that he had married Serena Jerome when they were both very young and that his wife had died in the same car accident that had killed his father-in-law. He still wore his plain gold wedding band on his left hand, which suggested to Harriet that he was perfectly content with his widowed status.

'I haven't.' A faint gleam of wry amusement thawed the blue frost in his eyes. 'Nicola assures me she's no longer a dependent child but an independent young adult.'

Harriet stayed silent as he paused expectantly. What did he want her to say to that? Why didn't he just get it over with so that they could get on with the business at hand? She was dying to find out what his urgent new project was, and whether it would mop up some of her seething energy. She shifted in the chair and tugged absently at the hem of her skirt. His eyes dropped and she was immediately made conscious of the absurdity of the gesture. No amount of tugging was going to make the skirt modest.

'Nicola is home on holiday at the moment and has apparently decided that, as a newly fledged adult, she needs to test the boundaries of her freedom.' He lifted his eyes to hers again, and Harriet was struck by their renewed coolness. Did he think that she had deliberately drawn his attention to her legs?

'Good on her,' she muttered, smitten by a deep sense of injustice. Why would she want to flaunt her legs at a man to whom fun was an alien concept? He was flattering himself if he thought that she would bother to try and vamp *him*. Marcus Fox was most emphatically not the type of man she was looking for to enliven her existence. He might be attractive in a grim sort of way but he reminded her too much of Keith. Her ex-fiancé had been solid, pragmatic and unsentimental, possessed of a pessimism that he had preferred to call realism and a mistrust of open emotion which had slowly crushed all spontaneity out of their relationship.

Marcus Fox frowned. 'As I said, she's only fifteen. Far too young to do the things she says she wants to do.'

'What kind of things?' Harriet asked, interested in spite of herself. Anything that had a hint of rebellion about it interested her these days.

'Drop out of school. Get a job. Date...'

Harriet blinked. At fifteen the girl wouldn't even have minimal qualifications yet, nor was she legally allowed to leave school. Marcus Fox, pillar of rectitude, the father of a teenage drop-out? No, that didn't fit the image at all! Doubtless he had fixed ideas for his daughter's future and she was kicking against the strait-jacket of his expectations. Go for it, Nicola, she urged silently, her full mouth curving at the idea of someone else out there making her reckless bid for freedom.

He leaned across the desk. 'You find something funny in all this, Miss Smith?' he demanded with lethal softness.

'No, sir.' She straightened her mouth hurriedly.

'Then what were you grinning at?'

'I wasn't grinning, sir.'

'Oh?' He challenged the flagrant lie. 'Then what *were* you doing?'

She had got into a rhythm now. 'Thinking, sir.'

'What about? And stop sirring me like that!'

'Like what, sir?' she asked innocently.

'Like *that*!'

'But I've always called you sir before,' she pointed out reasonably.

'You've always been a brunette before too, but you obviously had no trouble in changing *that*!' His expression stiffened in self-reproach and Harriet realised that he regretted his reference to her changed appearance.

'Actually it took a great deal of trouble.' She pounced on the slip. 'Don't you like my new look?'

'I hadn't considered it one way or the other,' he said crushingly.

'Then my information was obviously at fault.'

'What information?'

She couldn't back down now. She fluffed her curls with the kind of self-consciously feminine gesture that she had formerly despised. 'That you're allergic to blondes.'

Retribution was as swift as it was shatteringly unexpected.

'Only in bed.'

Harriet's hand fell back into her lap and she went poppy-red.

Suddenly much of the knotted tension drained out of the taut body behind the desk. Marcus Fox leaned back in his chair and chuckled, the hard angles of his face relaxing, his eyes warming to a shade of blue very close to her own as he studied her blush. His body swivelled back and forth with a lazy movement of his chair, his gaze the only fixed point in a suddenly vertiginous universe.

Laughing blue eyes.

Harriet was disorientated by a vague sense of *déjà vu*, but when she tried to pin down the feeling of familiarity her stomach began to squirm, prompting her to snap unwisely, 'What's so funny?'

He sobered. 'Why, nothing, Miss Smith. I was just thinking, Miss Smith...'

His parody of her taunting servility was perfect. He was laughing at her! The squirmy sensation vanished as red mist formed in front of Harriet's eyes. How easily he had vanquished her bold pretensions to sophistication! She throttled her rage, savagely willing her blush to recede. After months of listlessness these violent swings of emotion she was experiencing were slightly alarming. But at least they proved she was *alive*.

'About your errant daughter, no doubt,' she choked.

He inclined his head in mocking acknowledgement of her tacit surrender and remarked complacently, 'Not errant. Far from it. Nicola has always been willing to be guided by me and I don't think that this occasion is going to turn out to be any different...if it's handled correctly.'

'Which of course it will be.' Her sarcasm was obviously too subtle, for it went right over his annoyingly smug head.

'That's up to you.'

'To *me*?' Harriet sat up straighter. Her handbag slithered unnoticed to the floor as she tensed against an unwelcome premonition. 'What do you mean, it's up to me?'

'Nicola attends a school out of Auckland and normally during her holidays she goes away with my mother-in-law, Susan, but unfortunately Susan hasn't been well recently. She visited her doctor on Friday and he's suggested an urgent rest cure. She'll be absent for most of the holiday but she doesn't like the idea of leaving Nicola totally to her own devices for a fortnight, and neither do I.

'Unhappily her three closest friends are holidaying with their families overseas and I have no other relatives that I can ask to fill the breach—Nicola threatened outright rebellion if I humiliated her by employing a nanny or teacher to look after her. However, I have to take some positive action to stop Susan worrying. She's been an exemplary grandmother—has virtually brought up Nicola since she was five years old—and I won't have her suffering the added stress of feeling guilty for putting her own health first this once.'

'I still don't see what all this has to do with me,' murmured Harriet, her wariness increasing in direct proportion to his unprecedented expansiveness. He was marshalling his facts like a general amassing an army, their staunchly ordered ranks set to march ruthlessly over any hint of opposition.

'You will. Nicola has always been a fair student but she arrived home at the weekend acting moody and rebellious. She says that she's bored with studying and wants to leave school as soon as she legally can. On the other hand she freely admits that she has no idea what she wants to do with the rest of her life.

'I hope it's merely a disruptive phase she's going through, a resentment of authority in general, but, just in case it's not, this situation with Susan gives me the opportunity to kill two birds with one stone—keep Nicola fully occupied during the holidays and give her some experience of what it's like to work for a living. I'd like her to find out for herself that without specialist skills or qualifications, or ambitions, a job can be just as unexciting and restrictive as school. I want to be sure that any permanent decision she makes regarding her future is based on reality, not some rosy-eyed vision of adulthood as all freedom and no responsibility...'

'So you're going to let her get a holiday job?' Harriet guessed.

'I'm going to *give* her one,' he corrected her. 'At Trident. And that's where you come in.'

'You want me to find something for her to do?' Harriet said, relieved at the simplicity of his request. Her premonition had obviously been false.

'I've already organised that. Filing. She'll be transferring the old paper insurance records to the new filing system in the records room.'

Harriet nibbled her lip and grimaced faintly at the waxy taste of her new lip-gloss. '*Filing?* You mean that's all she'll be doing—shifting paperwork from one place to another?'

'It's a job that has to be done by someone, some time, and there's certainly enough work to keep her busy for a couple of weeks.'

'Yes, but wouldn't it be more educational to give her duties in the general office so that she can see the variety of skills she might need—'

'As Nicola herself has declared, she's fed up with being educated,' he said drily. 'I'm giving her what she says she wants—a job commensurate with her skills.'

'But filing day in and day out for two straight weeks!' Harriet shuddered at the thought. 'Even our office juniors get rotated on that kind of deadly dull work.'

'Our office juniors are more qualified than my daughter,' he pointed out.

'Surely she can type?' Since the advent of computers in classrooms, most children had at least rudimentary keyboard skills.

'Yes, but she thinks it's boring.'

'Wait until she discovers the joys of filing,' Harriet told him tartly. 'She'll be begging you for the thrill of typing.'

'Exactly. Except she'll have to follow office protocol like everyone else and go through the proper channels, so it'll be Miss Smith she'll be going begging to, not Daddy. You'll be her supervisor while she's here. In fact I want you to take her under your wing, treat her as if she was one of your protégées. Don't take any nonsense—make sure she understands that you expect her to meet certain standards of work and behaviour, and don't let her take advantage of the fact that she's the boss's daughter. At least not during office hours...'

Harriet listened with rising indignation as he blandly continued to expropriate her of her life.

'Nicola hasn't spent much time in Auckland recently and she won't know anyone else at work so I want you to befriend her, keep her busy during her lunch-hour—show her around... You could take her to a few cafés around the city, maybe visit some art galleries, show her the harbour, take her shopping... things like that. I'll arrange a company credit card for you and naturally I'll reimburse you for your time.'

Harriet was rigid in her chair, aghast at what this would do to her precious, new-found personal freedom.

'She's *your* daughter; why don't *you* spend your lunch-hours escorting her around town?' she blurted out.

'Because, unlike my waged employees, I don't *have* regular lunch-hours,' he said crisply. 'I have a very tight schedule over the next few weeks. If I do eat out it'll be at business luncheons. Nicola would be bored to tears—'

'I thought that was the general idea.'

He gave her an old-fashioned look. 'Don't be impertinent, Miss Smith.'

Impertinent! She'd give him impertinence! Harriet's eyes narrowed to dangerous slits.

'Let me get this straight. This is what you got me up here for? *This* is the special project for which you told Mr Jessop you needed my urgent help? You want to use me as a *babysitter*?'

'I wouldn't call it babysitting,' he asserted mildly.

'I don't care what *words* you use; it amounts to the same thing! You're asking me to be your daughter's chaperon from nine o'clock to five every day, to be responsible for her personal welfare. You can't be *serious*!'

He planted his palms flat on the desk in front of him, unperturbed by this display of rebellion. 'I wasn't *asking* . . . and I assure you, Miss Smith, I'm perfectly serious.'

She was horrified to see that he was. The humour had vanished from his blue eyes, replaced by a cool determination. 'But I don't *want* to do it!'

'Irrelevant.'

Regrettably she realised that he was right. She had never been asked before whether she *wanted* a particular task or not. Why should this one be any different? She clenched her small hands in her lap, seething with frustration. 'Surely there's someone more suitable, someone nearer her own age—?'

'I want someone mature—someone I know personally and whom I can trust. Come, Miss Smith, there's obviously no one more suitable than you—you're already in my employ, you're available on short notice and you're a sensible, level-headed lady who relates very well to the young people on the staff. They like you. They respect you. So will Nicola.'

Harriet's heart sank. He had certainly done his wretched homework. 'Lady'. 'Sensible'. 'Level-headed'. If she didn't stand firm in her resolution those words would be her epitaph.

She shuddered as the familiar trapped feeling began to close in on her. The hard, smothering pressure that made it difficult to breathe, let alone articulate.

'Why can't Miss Broadbent do it? Or what about your other private secretary?' she croaked desperately. 'She often works for you at your home, so Nicola must be used to having her around—'

'Miss Broadbent is too old and Miss Allison is in Italy on her honeymoon. She's taken advantage of the current lull in my overseas schedule to get married and I don't think her new husband would appreciate my recalling her for a less than life-or-death crisis. No, Miss Smith, I've already made up my mind.'

He had made up his mind. As if that settled the matter for all eternity!

'And what work am *I* supposed to be doing while your daughter is nodding over the files?' she said helplessly, visualising her vibrant, colourful, sexy new self withering away for lack of exposure.

'Don't worry, I don't expect you to share the mundane burden,' he offered in meagre compensation. 'That would be a foolish waste of human resources. I've had an extra computer terminal installed in the file room and Miss Broadbent has a couple of research projects that you should find both interesting and challenging—'

'Isn't that dangerous? What if Nicola looks over my shoulder and stops yawning?' she sniped.

'Then you can tell her about the secretarial course you graduated from with top marks in your class,' he replied with the glibness of one who had her personnel file open on the desk in front of him. 'If Nicola decides that office work might be her *métier* after all she could do no better than to take on you as a role model...'

If he expected her to be flattered he was mistaken. His compliment was the last straw.

'Role model! Are you *crazy*?' Harriet exploded to her feet, spreading her arms angrily so that her unbuttoned jacket parted over the filmy white blouse. '*Look* at me, for goodness' sake! Do I *look* as if I'm a suitable role model for a vulnerable young teenager? I'm the *last* person you should be asking.'

He stroked his chin in a characteristic gesture of patience. 'Calm down, Miss Smith—'

'No, I won't calm down. I don't want to calm down!' She was aware that her soft voice had risen shrilly and didn't care. She stood aggressively in front of his desk, her hands on her hips in defiance of his authority.

'Whatever you *think* you know about me, you're wrong. You're way out of date! Sure, I may be level-headed at work but in my own time I'm really quite irresponsible...I wouldn't be a good influence on your daughter at all. I'm not good with children and it's certainly not my idea of fun to spend my free time trailing around with some bored, rich brat and acting as if I care what she does. I'd probably lose track of her. I'm busy in my lunch-hours too, you know. I have places of my own to go, things to do, people to see...'

She trailed off as she saw that, instead of appearing disenchanted by her feverish claim to moral weakness and the insulting reference to his daughter, Marcus Fox was looking disconcertingly intrigued.

'Places to go?'

She scowled as she tried to think of somewhere suitably depraved. 'Yes—like the pub.' That was one of the first items on her 'must do' list. She had never been into the public bar of a hotel and had the outdated impression that they were smoke-filled dens of iniquity. 'Surely you wouldn't want your under-age daughter hanging around licensed premises with me? She might get arrested.'

Again she failed miserably to shock him. 'If you can't do without your daily tipple then you can have it at a licensed restaurant—I have no objection to you enjoying a drink with your lunch providing that you don't do it to excess, and that Nicola sticks to non-alcoholic fare. As I said before, I'll meet all the expenses involved—'

'What if I order champagne with every meal?' Harriet demanded wildly.

'More than one bottle at a time would be considered excessive,' he murmured.

Was he making a *joke*? Harriet eyed his unsmiling face warily. He returned her look blandly, but there was a certain implacable set to his wide mouth which made her realise that however much she squirmed he had no intention of letting her wriggle off his firmly baited hook.

'What if I just flat out refused?' she queried defiantly.

'Then I would suggest that you go away and read the small print on your employment contract before making a final decision.'

In the face of such a silken challenge Harriet was very nearly tempted. After all, her financial position was now such that she could afford to fling her resignation in his face on a mere matter of principle.

But something held her back. Maybe it was the calming influence of his cool, steady gaze, maybe it was the way his deep voice had gentled when he'd mentioned his rebellious daughter... or maybe she was just afraid of the frightening void which might open up in her life if she didn't have her familiar job to go to every morning. A life of unrelieved frivolity could prove to be as much of a trap as one of unrelenting routine, especially to the inexperienced.

It wasn't cowardice, Harriet told herself; it was a matter of taking control. She would leave when *she* was ready, and not a moment before.

'I still say you're making a mistake,' she said haughtily, attempting to save a modicum of face. 'Just remember, if anything goes wrong, I *did* try to talk you out of it.'

'I never evade my responsibilities,' he replied with a quietness that inspired a deep unease in her breast. It sounded unsettlingly as if he was making a vow.

'Nor allow them to evade you,' she sighed, wondering whether his darling daughter was as wilful as her father. Maybe she was an over-protected little madam who thought she had Daddy wrapped around her spoiled little finger.

A spark of something she couldn't identify smouldered briefly in the blue eyes. 'Quite. Now—'

He rose abruptly from his chair and, against the tinted window, he was suddenly a dark, shadowy figure sweeping across her dazzled vision. Harriet's heart pulsed erratically in her ears and, even knowing that the width of the desk was between them, she instinctively shied away from his dominance, a slender heel catching against the chair-leg behind her as she did so, half wrenching her shoe from her foot and throwing her off balance.

She stumbled forward several steps, banging her hip as she ricocheted off the sharp corner of his desk. One windmilling hand clipped the eyepiece of the telescope and it teetered on its extended tripod. Harriet whipped around to clasp and steady it, letting out a small cry of pain as a bolt on one of the legs jammed into her knee.

'What on earth—?' Marcus Fox was there immediately, untangling her from the apparatus and setting them both upright.

'I'm sorry,' she gasped, hopping on one leg as she tried to refit her shoe.

He let go of the telescope to support her by her shoulders, half lifting her with easy strength to perch on the edge of his desk while she fumbled. 'Little fool,' he said gruffly. 'What are you wearing heels like that for around the office? You're an accident waiting to happen.'

'To stop people like you calling me little,' she huffed. 'And I... High heels make my legs look longer.' It had sounded far more effective in the shoe-saleswoman's plummy tones.

'Your legs are quite long enough .particularly in that skirt.' He touched her knee, making her gasp at the unexpected intimacy, but he was merely being as meticulous as usual. 'I'm afraid you've laddered your pantihose rather badly. I hope you've got a spare pair tucked away to change into; you can't go around all day looking like that.'

Harriet automatically lifted her leg to inspect the damage, and as she flexed her tender knee the run gained width and momentum, splitting audibly as it shot up under her skirt.

'They're not pantihose,' she said absently, thinking gloomily that it didn't take much to make expensive elegance look cheap and tacky. Maybe black hadn't been such a flattering choice after all.

'I beg your pardon?'

He hadn't moved and Harriet was acutely aware that he was standing between her legs, the fabric of his dark trousers brushing against the sensitive skin of the insides of her knees. This time the threat posed by his proximity was unnervingly real. He was overpoweringly close, his warmth radiating through her like an invisible touch, his clean male scent creating a curious disorder in her senses. He made her feel both fragile and vulnerable and she panicked lest he detect her irrational fear, rashly seeking to repulse him with offensive brashness.

'I said I'm not wearing pantihose. They're stockings. See?' She provocatively lifted her knee to press it against his hip, and flipped back her hem to reveal the lace-trimmed suspender that gripped the opaque band of her laddered stocking. A strip of smooth, naked thigh was also inadvertently revealed—a starkly erotic contrast to the black lingerie.

They were both still frozen by her unthinking audacity when the door to the office was suddenly flung open and a trio of vividly contrasting females sailed in, the leader of whom was already carolling gaily, 'Yes, I know you didn't want any interruptions but I told Miss Broadbent you'd make an exception for your mother-in-law, especially since I'm bringing you your darling daughter and your dear, sweet Lynne—'

There was a concerted feminine gasp as the group came to a ragged halt, and the honey-sweet voice curdled to an acid roar.

'*Marcus!* What in heaven's name do you think you're doing? Unhand that wretched woman at once!'

CHAPTER FOUR

HARRIET was beginning to think that she had been foolish to wear a backless gown on a date with a relentless womaniser.

She plucked Michael Fleet's crawling hand out of the fabric draped around the base of her spine and replaced it on the relative safety of her hip for what seemed like the hundredth time since they had stepped onto the dance-floor.

'Michael, do you have to hold me so tightly? I can't breathe!' Plastered against his chest, she received an unwelcome blast of alcohol fumes whenever he turned his face towards hers.

'S'awlright, sweetie; if you pass out I can give you the kiss of life...' He hugged her even more tightly and nuzzled a wet mouth suggestively against her neck.

Harriet sighed. The evening which had sparkled with such early promise had degenerated to the point where she was seriously considering ducking out on her partner.

It was ages since Harriet had been to see a play, and the glittering first-night comedy that Michael had taken her to had perfectly suited her frivolous mood. She had equally enjoyed being plied with elegant food, wine and flattery over their late supper. It had only been when they had moved on to the nightclub that her spirits had flagged. She had expected frenetic rock and uninhibited freestyle dancing, but Lizzie's turned out to cater to the city's more sophisticated night-owls and the live band was slow, bluesy and very much an encouragement to old-fashioned smooching on the dance-floor.

The trouble was that she didn't want to smooch...at least, not with Michael. He had been such an entertaining companion that Harriet had taken it for granted that there must be a physical attraction between them, but when he had taken her into his arms she had been disconcerted to feel not a single spark of excitement. Instead of being aroused by his slyly wandering touch, Harriet had discovered an unexpected ticklishness, her fits of nervous giggles effectively destroying the mood he was trying to set.

At first Michael had been appealingly good-natured about her lack of response, but as the night had worn on and he'd realised that she wasn't going to fake a desire she didn't feel in order to pander to his ego he had begun to laugh less and drink more. He glared aggressively at other men who came to ask her to dance and sulked if she accepted. It had got to the stage where Harriet was feeling distinctly threatened by his surliness, but at least when they were out on the dance-floor he wasn't drinking. Perhaps if she kept him dancing long enough he would sober up and accept her rejection with good grace.

His hand drifted down again and this time he wouldn't let her pull it away. They were in the midst of a discreetly nasty tussle when an imperious finger tapped Michael on the shoulder.

'Mind if I cut in?'

'Yes, I do. Buzz off and find your own woman,' growled Michael without looking round.

'Why don't we ask the lady for her preference?'

'Look, mate—' Michael swung Harriet clumsily around so that he could insult the interloper to his face. The rest of his sentence was abruptly choked off. 'Uh? Oh—'

'You don't mind, do you, Fleet?'

'Uh—sure...I mean, no, no—go right ahead...'
Michael cannoned into another couple as he hastily
stepped back from Harriet, his normal fluency deserting
him in his anxiety not to offend a powerful superior.
'I'll just...er...I guess I'll go and sit at the bar...'

Harriet stood stock-still, her face flushed with mingled
relief and dismay, as her erstwhile partner melted into
the surrounding crowd. Marcus Fox looked down at her
revealing expression with a wry smile. 'It certainly pays
to have influence,' he murmured.

'M-Mr Fox—fancy seeing you here,' she said feebly.

'Fancy,' he mocked. He held out his hand, palm up.
'Shall we dance, Miss Smith?'

Unfortunately Harriet was still too stunned by his appearance to think of refusing. Of all the ghastly coinci-
dences! she thought as she moved stiffly into the circle
of his arms.

Marcus Fox was the last person she'd expected to see
kicking up his heels in a trendy nightclub. He was also
the last person she *wanted* to see, the memory of the
uncomfortable scene she had precipitated in his office
that morning still appallingly vivid...

Being painted a scarlet woman by his mother-in-law
had been embarrassing enough, but it was the elegant-
to-her-eyeballs Lynne Foster who had truly made Harriet
bristle. His 'dear, sweet Lynne', who hadn't turned an
exquisitely coiffured hair at the sight of him inspecting
the underwear of a daring blonde.

'I'm a criminal lawyer,' she had told Harriet in a
crisply amused voice as Harriet had scrambled off the
desk in a flurry of awkwardness, brushing away the
masculine hands that became inexplicably tangled in her
efforts to drag down her skirt. 'I would never dream of
allowing circumstantial evidence to convict a client...or
a friend.' From the warm look she'd cast Marcus Fox it

had been obvious that he was very much included in the latter category.

'You can make a full and frank confession over dinner tonight, Marcus,' she had teased him complacently, her tone implying that she knew he would never do anything so unbelievably tacky, while at the same time subtly establishing her territorial rights. To Harriet, her amused condescension had been far more humiliating than Susan Jerome's scathing contempt. She had blushed to the roots of her pale hair.

As for the man in question, to Harriet's chagrin he had remained infuriatingly detached from her embarrassment. Ignoring his mother-in-law's quivering outrage, he had calmly introduced Harriet in glowing terms and then suggested that she go away and *tidy herself up*...for all the world as if they had been messily engaged in the very activity that Susan Jerome suspected.

To compound his sin, as she moved past him he lowered his voice to murmur, for Harriet's ears only, 'Caught in a compromising situation twice within an hour with two different men? That must surely be some kind of office record, Miss Smith...'

Since it was physically impossible for her to blush any harder than she was already doing, Harriet took petty revenge by pausing to ask in a loud voice loaded with coy innuendo, 'And do you want me to come back and finish our...*discussion* when your visitors have gone, Mr Fox?'

He punished her by replying with ineffable blandness, 'Why, no, I think you've satisfied me quite sufficiently for today, Miss Smith. Miss Broadbent will let you know when I want you again.'

'Miss *Smith*?' Susan Jerome's sceptical glare bored into Harriet as she beat a chastened retreat, clearly insinuating that the ubiquitous surname must be a blatant attempt at deception. 'One of your most experienced secretaries, you say, Marcus?' she rapped out. 'Experienced at *what*? one is entitled to wonder.'

Harriet was wondering too. From his brief description she had created a vague mental picture of Marcus Fox's mother-in-law as a delicate flower of womanhood—genteel, kind and devotedly maternal. This tall, square woman with her sharp grey eyes and even sharper voice wouldn't have looked out of place as a warder in a woman's prison. Her powder-blue suit was as severely cut as a uniform, for all it dripped with class, and her regimented, blue-rinsed curls failed to soften the formidable front. A prison pallor, the only hint of ill health in her upright bearing, completed the unfortunate impression.

Lynne Foster was the exact opposite—a voluptuous, dark-haired, dark-eyed beauty who made the most of her femininity while still managing to look impressively businesslike.

Standing next to her, Harriet's proposed new protégée was completely eclipsed, but that didn't seem to bother Nicola Fox. She was as quiet as a mouse, hanging back as she watched the interaction between the adults with unblinking green eyes. Her long fair hair hung in a plait down her back and she wore round wire spectacles that emphasised the smallness of her pale face. She wore a neat cotton dress and lace-up shoes with white ankle socks. She didn't smile when she was introduced to Harriet, but at least she politely shook hands, which was more than the two older women had offered to do.

As she slipped out the door Harriet heard Susan Jerome say dismissively, 'Really, Marcus, a man in your position can't be too careful of his reputation . . . especially with that sort—a pert little miss and no mistake! But listen, the reason we came is to tell you that Lynne and I have come up with a *splendid* idea for Nicola's holiday—'

'A pert little miss'. I suppose that's an improvement on 'that wretched woman'! thought Harriet ruefully as she was waylaid by Miss Broadbent and handed a set of neatly typed instructions.

Thankfully, following them had kept her well away from the chairman's office for the rest of the day. She'd spent the morning tying up loose ends with Brian Jessop and Barbara, and the afternoon setting up her new desk and computer-link in the file room. Apart from a few lowly clerks, her only visitor had been Miss Broadbent, who'd descended from on high to deliver a box of disks containing the confidential research data that Harriet would need, and a personal memo in a thick, mono-grammed envelope...

Harriet's hands had actually been shaking as she had ripped it open, half expecting to find a polite message informing her that her services would now no longer be required. But it appeared that Mrs Jerome's *splendid* idea' had not held sway, for in a beautifully precise, almost calligraphic hand Marcus Fox had written that his daughter would be starting work the next day, and could Harriet please present herself at eight-thirty a.m. *sharp* in the executive foyer to take her on the standard familiarisation tour for new employees.

'Having fun?' Marcus asked as they moved in among the dancers, and it took a moment for Harriet to realise that he was referring to their conversation in the lift that morning.

She tossed her head. 'I *was*.' Her blue eyes glittered defiantly under gold-dusted lids.

'I'm glad,' he murmured, his insincerity as bold as her lie. That settled, he placed his large hand lightly be-tween her shoulderblades and gently urged her into motion. Although he was scarcely touching her, Harriet felt the delicate friction of his palm against her bare skin as if it were a brand. She shivered.

'Are you cold?' His warm breath stirred the blonde curls over her temple, and as she stared fixedly at his upper chest she wished that she were still wearing heels instead of low, strappy sandals. She didn't like having to tilt her head to see his face; it made it impossible to conceal her own expression and he was far too shrewd at reading people.

'No, I'm quite warm.'

Too warm, in fact. And she had that squirmy sensation again—the one that had haunted her in his presence ever since that New Year interview, when he had shattered her perception of him as a remote demigod, exposing instead a real man who was capable of suffering the same confusion and uncertainty as everyone else. She hadn't wanted her perceptions altered. At that time she had looked on her workplace as her haven—safe, unemotional, the one controllable aspect of her life. It would have been more than she could have coped with to acknowledge that it, too, might change...

'You surprise me...considering how little there is to your dress—and the fact that it appears to be entirely made of metal,' he commented drily.

She looked down at the fine gold mesh that poured like viscous liquid over the curves of her body from the deeply slashed neckline to the asymmetrical hem that revealed most of one leg. The weight of the flared skirt swung with her movements, the flat metal links turning to molten fire as they caught the fragmented lights above the dance-floor.

Harriet had chosen the most wickedly exotic new dress she owned to celebrate her official launch as a giddy socialite. All right, so perhaps it had been rather *too* exotic for a woman who hadn't quite decided on the level of her sophistication, she conceded. Perhaps Michael wasn't entirely to blame for coming to the conclusion that the woman inside the look-how-sexy-I-am dress would be a push-over...

'But very *precious* metal,' she said lightly, refusing to dwell on her mistakes. 'I think it must have been priced by the gram,' she added, and named a price that had given her palpitations when she had agreed to pay it. It was as much as she had previously spent on clothes in a year! 'Do you think I got my money's worth?' she probed.

To her disappointment he looked unmoved by her daring. He looked down at the glamorous mask that she had carefully applied to match the dress. Her lipstick had been worn off by the constant worrying of her teeth and tongue in the last uncomfortable hour with Michael. Her naked lips were a lush pale pink, soft and vulnerable in contrast to the sultry slash of her painted eyes.

'Undoubtedly it'll prove a very wise investment if you continue to keep company with aggressive playboys like Fleet,' he commented drily. 'You may need the protection of high-fashion chain mail. Men who won't take no for an answer can be hard to fend off, even for the most experienced coquette.'

He was lecturing again! 'Coquette,' she mocked. 'What an old-fashioned word!'

'I'm an old-fashioned man. I happen to believe that men should respect women—'

'Even blonde bimbos?'

His stern mouth took on a definite slant. He waited a few turns before murmuring, 'You do seem to be fixated with my attitude to blondes.'

Harriet shied away from any suggestion of personal interest. 'Only because I suppose that in the last twelve hours I've confirmed all your ridiculous prejudices!' she said carelessly.

'Actually, you've exploded a few of them.' His smile showed teeth as he invited, 'Would you like to know which ones?'

Panic curled around her throat and the hand resting on his left shoulder clenched unconsciously into a fist. 'No!'

A slight turn of his head, and his incisive jaw brushed against her white knuckles. 'Afraid?'

She shrugged haughtily in a shimmer of gold, composing her face into a look of intense boredom. 'No, merely uninterested.'

He chuckled admiringly. 'Oh, you do that very well.'

'Do what?'

'That look of magnificent disdain. As if I'd crawled out from under a slimy stone. Very crushing. Very *blonde*. Why didn't you look at Fleet like that, instead of letting him paw you all over the floor?'

'Maybe because I liked what he was doing,' she shot back.

'It certainly didn't look that way. He wouldn't have used such crude tactics if he knew you were willing. You were so busy keeping track of his hands, you didn't seem to notice that he was bulldozing you towards a dark corner.'

He must have been watching her for some time without her realising it. Even though they were in public it seemed like a disturbing violation of her privacy. 'I was handling it—'

'You were putting up with it. Quite a different thing. You were being far too polite, Harriet. You should have screamed, or slapped his face.'

Her name on his tongue almost distracted her from her annoyance. The aspiration was soft, the stress on the first syllable a deep purr, trailing off to a tiny click on the final consonant that caressed her with its haunting familiarity. 'Thank you, but I don't need your advice—'

'You need it; you just don't want it—'

'Don't presume to tell me what I want!' she flared. 'You don't know anything about it. I'm not under your jurisdiction here, you know. Outside working hours, Mr Fox, I'm just as much a free citizen as you are.'

'I think you'd better call me Marcus, don't you? Over the next couple of weeks you're going to be almost one of the family. Referring to me as Mr Fox in front of my daughter would be awkward for both of you—and Nicola might see it as an indication of your lack of authority. Far better for you to wield the subtle advantage of being on first-name terms with me.'

Her recoil was automatic. 'One of the family'? She looked up at him, shaking her head vehemently. 'Oh, I couldn't...'

'Why not?'

She floundered. 'Well, I— It wouldn't be—'

'Proper?' he supplied helpfully, steering her around the couple passionately kissing in the centre of the dance-floor. 'Of course; I understand completely. Very sensible of you to avoid any suggestion of impropriety. You have your own personal standards to uphold, and very worthy they are too. I don't blame you for worrying about what other people might think of your relaxation of your unwritten rules. A lady must protect her reputation, after all—'

'Not if she's building herself a brand-new one—*Marcus*,' she blazed, goaded to the limit by his kind understanding of her boring old self. 'What other people think is their own problem!'

'Precisely my view—Harriet,' he agreed, so smoothly that she arched her back to glare up at him and realised from his smug expression that she had just been skilfully manipulated. 'Now that we've got rid of that formality, perhaps we might be able to get to know each other a little better.'

At his innocuous comment a bloom of perspiration inexplicably mantled her skin and her hand suddenly felt slippery in his. Brief, unformed images danced before her eyes and she fought back a wave of smothering anxiety.

She looked away, unable to sustain her intent blue gaze, and laughed nervously. 'Perhaps, but I doubt it. We move in different circles. Yours is very much more formal . . .'

'Only sometimes. I'm dressed the way I am because we've just come from a first-night performance of the NZSO at the Aotea Centre.'

'We?' She tensed. Of course, he wouldn't be here alone. . .

'I had dinner and went to the concert with several friends. We have a table over there.' He gestured with an inclination of his head. Harriet followed the line of his sight and made a clumsy misstep as she recognised one of the figures seated at the edge of the dance-floor. The woman was frowning in their direction.

'You're here with Miss Foster,' she realised hollowly.

Marcus cushioned her slight stumble and a swirl of gold mesh wrapped itself briefly around the black fabric at his calf. He paused to allow its momentum to carry it free again, the hand on her back moving down to support her centre of gravity with a firmer pressure as he resumed his rhythm.

'Not as such, no. As I said, a group of friends had arranged to go to a charity dinner and then to the concert,' he said. 'Lynne happened to be one of them.'

'I'll bet she did,' muttered Harriet under her breath, remembering the way she had had her nose discreetly rubbed in the fact that they were dining together. A surge of rebellion coursed through her and she looked across and waggled her fingers over his shoulder at the haughty beauty watching them.

'That was uncalled for,' he murmured without looking down.

'I was just saying hello,' said Harriet innocently, smiling secretly to herself.

'You were taunting her.'

'I caught her eye. It would have been rude to ignore her,' she protested. 'All I did was wave.'

'It was the *way* you waved.'

'Oh, and how did I wave?'

'Provocatively.'

She laughed huskily, making her dress shimmer. She suddenly felt wicked, wild and abandoned...all the things that Michael had failed to make her feel. 'But I'm a provocative sort of woman,' she said headily. 'I like stirring things up. I'm irresponsible. I told you that this morning. Maybe now you'll believe me.' She peeped up at him through her sweeping false lashes and saw that he was looking satisfyingly stern.

'I believe you've had a little more to drink than you're used to. Fleet was probably topping up your glass when you weren't looking.'

'Of course he was! I'm not *stupid*, you know. And I'm not drunk, either!' At first she had let Michael get away with it because she'd thought that alcohol might help shake off her stubbornly persistent inhibitions. When she had realised that it wasn't working she had stopped going along with the game, and for the past couple of hours had merely toyed with her drinks.

'I didn't say you were,' he said diplomatically. 'Just that in your elevated mood you may be more vulnerable than you might think.'

Harriet's glossy new image was supposed to make her *in*vulnerable. Shallow, happy-go-lucky pleasure-seekers never got hurt... Look at Michael—he was annoyed with her but he wasn't emotionally wounded by her rejection. Harriet repressed a flutter of panic by scintillating even more brilliantly.

'If you mean I'm open to temptation, I hope so,' she said with a hectic little laugh. 'I like to make myself available to new experiences. It's so boring to just do the same things over and over again, don't you think?'

'It depends what those things are,' he murmured unco-operatively, the long, sensitive fingers that controlled her movements registering the rise in febrile tension in her slender body. 'After your experience at New Year I would have thought you'd be well aware of the insidious effects of alcohol.'

She might have known he'd bring that wretched topic up. He seemed obsessed by it.

'It's only insidious if you don't know it's happening. You should stop worrying about what happened at New Year. Everyone knows it wasn't the company's fault. And nobody really got hurt, except for their dignity, did they?'

'The fact that you need to ask makes the question debatable. There were a number of people in the same position as you that night. If you can't even remember what happened to you, how can you judge the extent of your hurt?'

'I meant lasting damage,' she said dismissively. Several of her workmates had mentioned how maudlin she had been in her intoxicated state, but that seemed to have been the extent of her foolishness. Thank goodness she hadn't broken down completely...not in public, anyway.

She remembered staggering into a dark, empty office, feeling wretched, there to wallow in self-pity, weeping herself into a fitful sleep that was menaced by jumbled hallucinations which, from her vague remembrance, seemed to involve an angel and a devil fighting for possession of her body and soul. Fortunately the angel must have won, because the darkness had rolled back in a burst of glory that had warmed the rest of her dreamless slumber. Somehow in the wee small hours she must have tottered out and got a taxi home and, since January the first was a holiday, she had gratefully spent the rest of the day in bed, recovering from what she had naïvely thought was a bout of food poisoning.

'Damage doesn't have to be physical to be lasting. Who knows what wounds may be hidden in the psyche?'

Harriet shrugged. The discussion was getting uncomfortably close to intense. Why did he persist in talking about an incident that everyone else was very happy to forget? 'As long as they stay hidden, who cares? What people don't know can't hurt them.'

There was a grim set to his jaw. 'That sort of philosophy has a nasty habit of backfiring.'

'Oh, well, if you want to talk on deep, meaningful topics like philosophy, then I've definitely had too much to drink,' she said, searching desperately for a diversion. 'Why don't you ask your "dear, sweet Lynne" to dance? She looks willing to be deep and meaningful, and she's obviously as sober as a judge.' Dressed in basic black, she looked like one too, thought Harriet nastily, although the beautiful legal eagle would no doubt take that as a compliment!

'Because I'm dancing with you.'

She mistrusted the gallantry. 'What kind of answer is that?'

'What kind of question was it? If you want to know what kind of relationship Lynne and I have, why don't you just ask?'

Her eyes jerked to his, sparkling defiantly. 'And be accused of impertinence again?' she charged.

'I got the impression this morning that being impertinent was one of your new aims in life,' he said shrewdly. 'However, if you're too shy to ask, I'll tell you: a useful one. Lynne and I have been dating casually for the last few months...mostly a matter of attending public events together when our schedules permit. Neither of us has any claim on the other.'

Brilliant natural colour flared under the smooth application of her glamorous make-up as Harriet realised what he meant. 'Why should I care?'

'Curiosity, perhaps?'

'Curiosity killed the cat.' And as soon as the stupid cliché was out of her mouth Harriet went white and closed her eyes, a horrified expression on her face.

'What's the matter?' he murmured deeply, bowing his head so that it almost touched hers.

Harriet shook her head, her hair flaring around her slender neck, releasing a cloud of heavily sensual perfume that made his nostrils flare. The fingers of his right hand shifted, interweaving through hers and folding down over her knuckles in a strong, reassuring grip. 'What is it, Harriet?'

'Nothing.' It came out as an anguished whisper.

'I don't believe that. Why are you looking like that? Tell me what's wrong,' he said in a voice so gentle that she wanted to lean on it and be softly enfolded in its promise of peace.

'Nothing!' She said it again, more strongly, opening eyes that were suddenly burning with rage. She tossed her head, almost hitting him on the jaw. 'Nothing. Nothing is *wrong* except that I'm dancing with a man whose girlfriend is glaring daggers at me! If you want to make her jealous, why don't you go and foist your company on someone else?'

He deftly spun her around, so that she could no longer see Lynne Foster craning at them from her chair. 'It's more likely to be me she's glaring at,' he said quietly, absorbing her anger with his calm. 'I've upset her by not being my usual agreeable self, but I don't intend to raise expectations I can't fulfil. And I'm afraid that she thinks I'm stubborn and uncooperative because I was so rude to Susan this morning—'

'You were rude to your mother-in-law?' Harriet blurted out.

'I agree—hardly the actions of a gentleman,' he said with a wry humour that further blunted the jagged edge of her pain. 'Perhaps I'll be blackballed from my club.'

Harriet's taut mouth almost trembled into a reluctant smile, and he relaxed some of his watchfulness to continue lightly, 'I'm afraid Susan is too used to getting her own way where I'm concerned. It's my fault—I've found life is much easier if I let her think she can organise me to her own satisfaction. This morning, for example, she wanted me to agree to Nicola working for Lynne at her law office during the holidays.'

Harriet caught her breath. 'But hadn't you told her that you were arranging for Nicola to have a job at Trident?'

He raised rueful eyebrows. 'When dealing with Susan it usually saves a lot of time and argument if I present her with a *fait accompli*. I had intended to do that tonight when I'd confirmed the arrangements, but unfortunately she saw fit to launch a pre-emptive strike—'

It seemed a very good description of Susan Jerome's approach. 'But—it's a terrific idea, isn't it?' Harriet interrupted feverishly. 'And it means that you won't need me after all...'

'It means I need you all the more. I'm afraid Susan's plan has the potential to create a bigger problem than it solves,' he said, firmly squashing any hopes she might have had of evading her responsibilities.

'What problem?' she asked, for the second time that night failing to realise that she was being danced into a corner, this time figuratively.

His jaw tightened. 'It's rather embarrassing...'

'Is it?' She wouldn't have thought, from the way he had handled himself this morning, that Marcus was capable of being embarrassed about anything. She wondered whether it was something a reckless woman might be able to use to her advantage. 'In what way?' she asked eagerly, then flushed when he gave her an ironic look, as if he knew exactly what she was thinking.

'Susan and her infernal matchmaking. She thinks that it's time I was respectably remarried and she's decided that Lynne fits the bill. I suspect that she cooked up this law office deal on the spur of the moment as a way of throwing us together as a cosy family unit, to impress me with Lynne's supportiveness—making time in her busy, successful career for Nicola's and my sake et cetera, et cetera. Susan obviously expects propinquity to succeed where natural inclination has failed.'

His eyes narrowed as he looked over her shoulder and Harriet was glad that his glacial look wasn't directed at her. 'Lynne is far too intelligent a woman not to have realised by now what Susan is up to, so I have to assume that she's operating on her own agenda. If I hadn't nipped the idea in the bud I feel I would have been tacitly acknowledging a level of commitment between us that doesn't exist. Fortunately, since I had a logical and far more convenient alternative already arranged, everyone's pride has remained more or less intact...'

'What about Nicola? She's the most important one in all this. What did *she* have to say?' Harriet asked tartly, to conceal the kick of petty satisfaction she felt at his cool dismissal of the lovely Lynne.

There was something deliciously amusing, too, in the idea of the powerful Marcus Fox being harassed by a matchmaking mama-in-law and trying to evade the acquisitive instincts of pursuing females. It made him seem less...threatening. Maybe she would be able to squeeze some fun out of the situation after all!

'Nothing, to Susan's annoyance,' he remarked drily. 'Nicola didn't seem to have an opinion either way, so naturally she accepted what I had arranged.'

Harriet didn't think that that sounded very rebellious. 'And did you tell Mrs Jerome that *I* was the one who was going to be in charge of Nicola?'

He looked her straight in the eye, blue on blue. 'I told her that it would be someone I trusted implicitly. She was content to accept my assurance.'

'You didn't tell her!' she breathed, realising suddenly that she could read that poker-face.

He quickened his steps to the beat of the music as it built smoothly in a crescendo. 'I said that she could go away happy in the knowledge that Nicola was going to be close under my direction.'

'You didn't tell her,' she reiterated gleefully as she was whisked into a series of dazzling turns that blurred everything but her partner's boldly delineated face into oblivion. 'You were too afraid to!'

'I obeyed the doctor's orders and removed a source of tension and worry that would have impeded her recovery,' he corrected her.

'Coward!' she laughed as she followed him through another whirlwind of steps, exhilarated by her ability to sense his every move. Her dance skills were very rusty and with Michael she'd had to concentrate on which foot went where. Marcus kept her too preoccupied to worry about such mundane issues and in his arms she rediscovered a soaring sense of freedom. Her erratic spirits shot skywards again, showering her with sparks of ridiculous joy.

'I freely admit to being henpecked,' he said, bringing her to a flourishing stop beside a rounded pillar as the band finished their set.

'And here was I thinking you were cock of the walk,' she said impulsively, and blushed when his answering smile imbued her words with a slightly indecent connotation she hadn't intended. Now he had made her aware of his body again . . . his whole body this time, not just its polite outer sheath of expensive black and white silk.

Like a flash photograph it etched itself momentarily on her retina, searing her with its vividly imagined detail—the column of his throat flowing down to a chest of tanned satin, smooth and hairless, a ripple of muscle beneath the arch of his ribcage dropping away to the breathtaking splendour of his masculine pride, and the flat hips and long, hard thighs, the slender, elegant feet...

'Pompous and strutting?' His thick black brows rose imperiously above the mocking smile. 'Is that what you think of me, Harriet?'

'If the cap fits,' she replied weakly, not moving as his hands dropped away, shocked by her own prurience. She had never stripped a man with her eyes before and it had happened almost without her volition. With such an unlikely subject, too. . . or should she say *object*? The colour burned in her cheeks. Maybe she *was* a little drunk. Or maybe it was just that her secret, sensual self was finally breaking through the taboos created by her gentle upbringing. She laughed breathlessly. It really was happening! The rebirth of Harriet Smith. All she had to do was look and act differently and soon she would be different.

'Harriet? I asked if you were ready to go home now.'

'What?' What was he talking about? Home was a dark, lonely house, aching with memories. Why would she want to go back there? Harriet turned fever-bright eyes up to his, her smile one of desperate gaiety. '*No!* No, of course not. What makes you say that? I'm having too much fun to leave!'

'The band is packing up soon, anyway,' he said, stilling the restless flutter of her hand by catching it in his own.

'This place only has a licence until one-thirty a.m. on week nights. And your sparkle is starting to tarnish. Come on; I'll give you a lift home.'

His gentle tone made her dig her heels in. He was being condescending and she didn't like it. 'No, Michael's doing that,' she insisted.

'I don't think your escort is in any condition to drive right now, do you?' He nodded to where Michael was leaning aggressively over the bar, arguing with the barman about the way he had made his drink.

'Then I'll drive—'

'*If* you could get his keys off him, and *if* he would let a mere woman drive that precious macho machine he calls a car, and *if* you hadn't had a few drinks yourself...'

Battered by his impeccable logic, she said the first stupid thing that came into her head. 'I came with him, I have to go home with him.'

'Don't be foolish—'

'It's not foolish; it's a simple matter of politeness.'

He gave a crack of grim laughter. 'And how polite do you think he's going to be when he gets you alone in his car? Or when you hit your doorstep? Polite enough to take no for an answer? A happy drunk is one thing, an angry drunk another. He certainly didn't seem very happy about the way you were holding him off. Michael is *not* a gracious loser.'

It was exactly what she had been worried about earlier, why she had several times refused Michael's suggestion that they leave. 'I can—'

'Handle it,' he finished tightly. 'So you keep saying. Tell me, do you *want* to go to bed with him tonight, Harriet?'

She flushed at his bluntness. He stood over her, tall, dark and grim. If she said yes he would go away and stop trying to ruin her enjoyment of life.

'I *was* going to say I can get a taxi,' she said haughtily. 'I can look after myself, you know; you don't have to feel responsible.' Her haughtiness deserted her as she looked over at her sullen escort and nibbled her lower lip. 'But I'll have to go over and say goodnight; I can't just desert him without a word... and he really should get a taxi himself...'

Marcus gave her an exasperated look. 'Old habits die hard, don't they, Harriet? The idea is not to give him the chance to object. Allow me to offer polite apologies on your behalf...'

CHAPTER FIVE

'I CAN'T believe you did that,' Harriet was muttering ten minutes later as they purred along the quiet motorway towards the suburbs.

'What? Got rid of Fleet for you?'

He had done more than that. He had confiscated Michael's car keys and arranged for the barman to call a taxi when he was ready to leave. All achieved with a minimum of discussion, from what Harriet could see from her cowardly vantage point beside the pillar.

'No, I mean...left your friends like that. What did you tell them?'

'That I'd found a hot blonde I was taking home for the night.'

She was too on edge to appreciate the subtle irony in his tone.

'You *didn't*!' She looked in horror at the bold profile, illuminated in jagged bursts by the streetlights whipping past the windows of the Volvo.

'Of course I didn't,' he murmured, casting her a chiding glance. 'What do you take me for?'

A consummate gentleman, of course. He would never be so crude as to embarrass a lady deliberately. Harriet was annoyed with herself for being so gullible.

'Then what *did* you say?'

'That I had extricated an employee from a difficult situation, that she was distressed and I was taking her home.'

'Miss Foster didn't look too pleased.' She tried hard to keep the satisfaction out of her voice. Since she scarcely knew the other woman it wasn't fair to dislike her so heartily.

He gave her a wry look that told her she hadn't quite succeeded. 'She wanted to come, but I suggested that, since you live on the opposite side of the city and it might take some time, it would be more sensible if she went home in the limo with the others.'

'But I hadn't told you where I lived—'

'I had your personnel file on my desk this morning, remember?'

'I'd rather not,' she blurted out involuntarily, but the reminder made her add cattily, 'I'm surprised she didn't insist on riding along as chaperon.'

'She tried to, but I said that I wanted to spare you any further embarrassment, that you preferred not to draw attention to your distress.'

'There was no need to make me sound like such a wimp,' she grumbled.

'There was every need. Why do you think I didn't invite you over there with me to say goodbye?' he said drily. 'At close range your status as a victim might be questionable, especially if you chose to make one of your unpredictable remarks. Damsels in distress don't normally wear skintight dresses or boast about their provocative behaviour.'

'So it was to save yourself embarrassment rather than me,' she said tartly. 'I suppose I'm not good enough to be introduced to your friends—'

'It depends in which context you use the word "good",' he said coolly. 'You certainly don't look *good* in that dress.'

Was he criticizing her for wearing something body-hugging when she didn't have much of a body to hug? She placed a defensive hand across her small breasts. She knew that she had grown far too thin over the past year. She had tried hard to eat wisely but it was almost impossible when your appetite was as depressed as your spirits.

But that, too, had changed over the weekend. Suddenly her taste buds were back in full cry, and tonight she had eaten three full courses while Michael had looked on in bemused wonder. At this rate she would soon have her former healthy shape back.

In the meantime she refused to allow Marcus to undermine her shaky confidence. 'Well, I happen to like the way I look!'

'You see what I meant about context? I simply meant that you're obviously flaunting the sultry, bad-girl look tonight. You don't look like the kind of woman who would be unduly distressed by the advances of an over-eager lover.'

'Michael Fleet is *not* my lover,' she denied, her hand clenching between her breasts, feeling her heart beat nervously against her knuckles. So he didn't think that she looked like a child masquerading as a woman. He didn't just see her as a silly little prude who had got out of her depth. He thought she looked sultry...sexy...

'Potential lover, then.'

'Not that either,' she said abruptly. 'I've decided that Michael's not really my type—'

'If you'll recall, I tried to point out to you this morning— '

'Don't you *dare* say I told you so!' she hissed.

He spun the wheel lightly between his hands as the powerful car took a long, fast curve, driving with the same calm confidence that he seemed to bring to every aspect of his life.

'I told you so.'

His soft words fell into the silence. She made an inarticulate sound under her breath.

'Well?' he enquired gently. 'Now that I've dared, Harriet, what do you intend to do about it?'

She ignored the taunt. 'Take this next exit,' she said, indicating the illuminated sign, 'or you'll have to go the long way round.'

He obeyed, swooping up the ramp and pulling up at the stop sign at the top, where he turned to look at her, resting an arm across the back of the seat behind her head.

'Be as provocative as you like, my dear, but don't dare a man to action unless you're prepared to deal with the consequences of his accepting the challenge. And remember, a dare doesn't necessarily have to be put into words to exist. The way you dress can be a very potent public challenge to a man to prove his masculinity. He might have a right to feel taken in by false advertising if a woman who chooses to wear something overtly sexual in his company proves indifferent to his sexual approaches. I can almost find it in me to feel sorry for Fleet...'

'Are you suggesting that I'm to blame for Michael's unseemly behaviour?' Harriet demanded raggedly, infuriated by that tacked-on remark.

'"Unseemly"?' His eyes glimmered at the primness of the word. '"Blame" is too strong a word, I think. But, whether you set out with that intention or not, you created a false expectation in him from the moment he first saw you in that dress.'

'Well, how was I to know that...that...?'

'That he would be so susceptible to your charms?' He sounded distinctly amused now. 'Why shouldn't he have been? He's a man who judges people by their appearance, and your charms do appear very...' his eyes wandered over the subdued glitter of her gown '...available.'

'He never acted like that before!'

'You never appealed to his susceptibilities before. So...was there a little revenge wrapped up in the mixed signals you were giving him tonight, Harriet? Beckoning him yet pushing him away? Were you punishing him for ignoring you in the past, for treating you as if you didn't exist as a woman? Or perhaps it was *all* men you were trying to punish...?'

She was ashamed to admit that there might be a grain of truth in what he said. 'I dressed the way I did tonight purely for my own enjoyment!'

'For fun?'

'Yes! Can we go now, or are we going to sit at this stop sign all night while you lecture me about things that are none of your business?'

'Where?'

What was he suggesting? That she might want to go somewhere else with him? Harriet's heart beat a little faster. 'Home, of course!'

'I mean which way do I turn?' he asked, returning both hands to the wheel.

'Oh.' Her heartbeat slowed and she hid her chagrin in her terse directions. 'Left, and then the second on the right.'

The rest of the short drive was accomplished in silence, and when he pulled up outside the gate and turned off the engine Harriet groped at her side for her mesh bag and muttered a hurried thank-you.

'My pleasure,' he replied courteously, making her feel like an ungrateful beast.

'And I'm sorry for ruining your evening,' she said contritely.

'Is that what you did?'

She was disconcerted by his murmured comment. 'Well, yes...of course. I mean...taking you away from your friends like that. But you could still go back to the nightclub—'

'Generous of you to suggest it, but they'll have left by now.'

'Oh, well...' Her fingers awkwardly pulled at the latch to release her seat belt. 'Were they going on somewhere? Perhaps you could catch them up.'

'I think that would be most unwise.'

'In what way?'

'I might have to answer all sorts of awkward questions about you. And I don't want to be seen to be rushing back to Lynne's side at the first opportunity. If I had been less...distracted....by other matters over these past couple of months I might have realised that between them she and Susan seem to have created the impression amongst my circle of acquaintances that we're an established couple. Tonight was supposed to be a casual intermingling of mutual friends of both sexes but Lynne managed to build something personal out of it by asking for a lift and thus pairing herself off with me. Perhaps this will help jolt people out of their misconceptions...'

It certainly gave Harriet a jolt. 'But you said you told them I was only an employee—'

His smile mocked her naïvety. 'And you think they believed that was really all there was to my knight-in-shining-armour act? Do you think that Lynne believed me, after the way she caught us out this morning?'

She froze. 'But she didn't catch us out. W-we weren't doing anything wrong,' she stammered.

'Of course we weren't,' he said in a soothing tone that had the opposite effect. He unsnapped his seat belt and she suddenly realised what he was doing.

'You don't have to bother to get out.' She scrabbled quickly for the doorhandle.

He was already out of the car. He bent to smile at her through his open door. 'Nonsense; my mother would be appalled by such a lack of manners.' He closed it with a solid clunk and strode around the bonnet to whisk hers out of her uncertain hand, impressing her yet again with the speed that seemed at odds with his contemplative character.

'Your mother's still alive?' she asked curiously, conscious as she swivelled in her seat that her outside leg was the one bared almost to the top of her thigh by the deeply asymmetrical hem of her skirt.

'Unfortunately no; she died not long after my marriage, but she placed great importance on politeness and respect for others, and her lessons will be with me all my life.'

There was a rich regret in his voice that spoke of deep esteem and an unashamed love. Was that why he was so kind and considerate towards Susan Jerome, so tolerant of her bossy interference in his life—because she had taken the place of his mother in his affections?

'And your father?' She ignored the hand he was holding out to assist her, asserting her independence by placing her sandals primly together on the concrete kerb and launching herself forwards and upwards with the momentum of her upper body.

'My father was an alcoholic who drank away every cent of a considerable inheritance and then conveniently fell ill so that the government would subsidise his booze. When he died I had to leave university to pay the debts he had run up. It was because of him, I think, that my mother set such store by manners and appearances; it was the only way she felt able to maintain her dignity in the face of increasing emotional and physical deprivation.'

The sweeping extent of his answer to so casual a question startled Harriet, as did the thinly veiled contempt for his father. She jerked her head up to look at him and the heel of one of her sandals caught in the sweeping point of her hem, sending her tumbling forward against his outstretched arm.

'I'm sorry!' she gasped, feeling her fingers dig into the straining muscle of his forearm as he took her full weight.

'Don't be. It was a long time ago,' he murmured as she quickly steadied herself and moved away.

'I meant—for grabbing at you like that.'

'Accepting a little help from time to time isn't a crime, Harriet. You don't have to do everything yourself.'

Little did he know, she thought bitterly.

'I—well, thank you for bringing me home.' She edged away towards the gate in the neat white picket fence that edged the footpath, and to her consternation he calmly followed, glancing up at the dark windows of the slightly shabby wooden house.

'I always see a lady to her door. There's no light on and you seem none too steady on your feet. You might hurt yourself in the dark.' He opened the gate for her. 'After you.'

She fumed as she went up the uneven pathway, her bare back prickling as she imagined that she could feel his warm breath puffing against her skin. Why did he have to walk so close? And why hadn't she left the porch light on? she wondered as she climbed the wooden steps, fumbling blindly in her bag for her keys. Because she had been too eager to leave, she remembered. She hadn't wanted Michael in the house, hadn't wanted to associate him in any way with her past.

'Oh, damn!' Now she had dropped them. Marcus stooped, the tips of his fingers brushing against her bare toes as he retrieved the dainty keyring and handed it back. She sorted through the keys by feel and then was chagrined to find that her hand was shaking so much that she couldn't get the right one in the blasted lock.

'Why in the hell won't the damned thing go in?' she said shrilly.

'Swearing at it won't help.'

'No, but it makes me feel better!' She swore again, to ensure that he knew she didn't care about his pious disapproval. She felt gratifyingly wicked. Another taboo broken!

'Well, if you're going to use bad language, at least be creative about it,' he drawled, and used a phrase to describe the recalcitrant lock and key that made Harriet blush hotly in the dark. The words seemed far more indecent coming from the polite mouth of Marcus Fox than they would have being uttered by a construction worker or docker.

To compound his offence he said with silky perception, 'I feel quite a glow coming from your direction. I haven't embarrassed you by any chance, have I, Harriet?'

'Of course not!' she said in her most worldly tone.

He hesitated, and then said quietly, 'Well, I still apologise for my indelicacy. It was an insult to both of us. I shouldn't have let you provoke me into sinking to your level.'

It seemed that even when he was being most gentlemanly he was being most insulting! 'You—'

'Careful; you're going to break it off, wrenching it like that. Here, give it to me.'

To her frustration the lock and key co-operated sweetly at his merest touch. Marcus stepped across the threshold and found the switch for the light without even fumbling.

'We won't wake anyone, will we?' he asked quietly, glancing down the softly illuminated hall. 'I know elderly people tend to be very light sleepers.'

'Elderly people?'

'Your parents.' He looked back in time to catch her still painfully off guard. 'This is your family home, isn't it? Your personnel file listed your parents as next of kin, living at the same address.'

To hide the shock that she was afraid he would see in her eyes, Harriet turned abruptly into the nearest room.

'Well, they don't now. I told you, your information is all out of date.' She turned on the light and dimly registered that they were in the cosy lounge where she had spent so much time playing, studying and reading over the years while her father sat in his chair and did his crosswords and her mother placidly knitted and worried about what Tim was up to with his high-spirited friends.

'Did your—?'

The question remained stillborn as he moved up behind her and saw the cartons and boxes and possessions strewn haphazardly around the room. It looked, Harriet knew, as if a bomb had exploded in their midst, and in a way it had...a human time bomb...

'What's happening here? Have you been robbed?' he demanded, moving protectively in front of her, righting a fallen lamp on the floor and straightening the broken shade.

'No, of course not. I'm packing everything up...I've sold the house.'

'*Sold* it?'

For some reason his startled tone made her feel defensive. She ran a careless hand through her platinum waves. 'Why shouldn't I? It's my house. It's such a waste in an area like this to have such a small house on a big section. It makes much more sense to pull it down and build several town houses on the same site—'

'Is that what you're going to do?' He interrupted her paean to modern town planning.

'Not me personally. A developer. He's had an offer in at the local real-estate office for ages and this weekend I finally decided to accept it. Would you like some coffee?'

He ignored her desperate offer of a social diversion. 'And what about your parents—what do they think about the idea?'

Harriet's polite smile held. 'I told you, the house is mine. I can do what I like with it. Are you sure you wouldn't like a cup of coffee?'

He stood there quietly, just looking at her with a patient, serious gaze that whittled away at her nerve. He would stand there like that all night if she didn't give him some sort of satisfaction.

'Look, I inherited it, if you must know,' she said. 'When my father died the house came to me.'

'Not your mother?' His thick brows drew together.

'My mother died quite some time ago... a stroke,' she said with deliberate vagueness, her voice devoid of emotion. 'After that Dad's health deteriorated and he was ill for a long while before his death.'

'But nobody altered the next-of-kin listing on your personnel file?'

She shrugged as if it had been an oversight rather than a subconscious act of denial. 'I didn't think of it and I don't suppose anyone else at work realised... I didn't need to ask for any compassionate leave because I was on holiday on both occasions.' She didn't say that she had requested holiday leave the second time because she'd known that her father was dying. No, more than that, he was *wanting* to die... to join the wife who had abandoned him to a downward spiral of depression and ill health.

'You preferred your bereavement to remain private; I can understand that.' For a grateful moment she thought that he was going to act on his respect for her feelings and drop the subject. 'But all the files were updated two years ago—this must all have been fairly recent...?'

'Not really. My father died—oh, last year some time,' she said, as if the exact date were not engraved deep on her heart. She looked down at her slender wrist before remembering that she wasn't wearing a watch. Time was another tyranny she had desired to escape. She twisted her hands behind her back and took a deep breath. 'Look, Mr—Marcus, it's very late and I'm tired—'

'You don't look it. You look restless and on edge, as if you're going to burst out of your skin.'

It was exactly how she felt. 'Do you blame me? I didn't expect to come home to an interrogation!' she said angrily.

'No, you're responsible only for yourself these days,' he said gently. 'No one wanting to know where you've been and with whom and what you did. Is this the first time you've lived alone, Harriet?'

'Yes. And I happen to like it!' she flared.

'Did I sound patronising?' he said quizzically. 'I didn't intend to. There's a first time for everyone and often the first time has a sweetness that's never matched. I envy you... it's a long time since I thrilled to the matchless enchantment of experiencing a simple new pleasure.'

She wondered what complicated pleasures it took to thrill him now. He hadn't been talking about sex but inevitably it was the most obvious experience that occurred to Harriet's over-stimulated imagination.

'So you feel that you've already tasted everything life has to offer?' she sniped sceptically, hoping that he would attribute her flustered reaction to annoyance.

'Not quite everything,' he murmured. 'Life does still manage to surprise me now and then. You certainly have.' He gave her one of his rare smiles. 'Did you say you were going to make some coffee?'

'I've changed my mind,' she said mistrustfully, and, to make certain he got the message, added, 'Besides, I think I've run out. Sorry.'

To her dismay he threw her insincere apology back in her teeth. 'Shall we have a look?'

Before she could stop him he was walking through the house, swiftly finding the disordered dining-room-cum-kitchen and, to her disbelief, starting to poke in various cupboards.

'It looks as if you've run out of most things,' he said, commenting on the lack of groceries in her pantry. 'Have you been eating properly? A lot of people who live alone find it a chore to cook for themselves.'

'I prefer to keep my food fresh in the fridge,' she said quickly, sensing another lecture, then blushed as he immediately turned, opened it, and surveyed the freakish results of her whirlwind visit to the supermarket the previous evening. She had jars of caviare and bars of chocolate, stuffed olives and plump Danish pastries, smoked salmon and Chinese pickles, and a dozen expensive cheeses all crammed in around bottles of cheap bubbly. She had shopped on the theory that if a little bit of what you fancied was good for you then a whole lot more must be even better.

'Do you mind? You're letting the cold air out.' She pushed the door shut with the flat of her hand, almost taking off the tip of his arrogant nose.

'A woman with eclectic tastes in food,' he merely remarked, turning to the bench, where he opened a canister to find the tea. 'Ah, just what we're looking for! I think tea is a better idea than coffee for anyone in your hyped-up state. It's an old wives' tale, you know, that coffee counteracts the effects of alcohol—'

'I'm not drunk,' she insisted for the second time that evening.

'No, but you're still a little wired.'

She watched helplessly as he found the teapot and cups and saucers, and plugged in the electric kettle. 'Make yourself at home,' she said sardonically.

'Thank you, I will,' he replied, leaning his shoulder against the cabinets beside her head and folding his arms across his chest, drawing the superbly tailored black dinner jacket tight over his broad shoulders.

'I was being sarcastic.'

'Loses its effectiveness somehow, doesn't it, when you have to point that out?' he mused. 'Would you like to slip into something more comfortable while the kettle boils?'

'I *beg* your pardon?' She gaped at him.

'That wasn't a euphemism for an indecent proposal, Harriet,' he said, amusement flashing like lightning in the blue eyes. 'That just doesn't look like the kind of dress you can relax and put your feet up in.'

'Since I'm not going to do either until you leave, it hardly matters what I'm wearing,' she said stiffly. 'I'm quite comfortable enough to drink a cup of tea!'

'So, when do you move out?' he asked, accepting the snub graciously.

Harriet grabbed at the blessed distraction and the chance to hammer home a point. 'As soon as I can find somewhere else to live. I *had* hoped that would be this week, but now that it seems my lunchtimes are going to be taken up with your daughter I suppose I'll have to leave my property-hunting to the evenings.'

'I don't see why. Nicola could be a great help. She likes seeing where other people live and she has excellent taste for one so young. She can give you a second opinion.'

Harriet could think of nothing worse than consulting someone else about *her* fantasy pad. 'I'm not looking for the kind of place that would appeal to a teenager. I want something sophisticated and...and...' she waved a hand expressively as she sought for the right word '...swinging.'

'*Swinging*?'

Her hand fluttered back to her side and she glared at his suspiciously straight face, conscious that her archaic slang had probably betrayed her abysmal ignorance of the life she was intent on pursuing. 'Somewhere I can meet lots of independent young people who like to party and enjoy the good things in life.'

'I see. You mean reckless, fun-loving people such as yourself.' He tilted his dark head, faint threads of grey gleaming in the thick black pelt as they caught the light, reminding her that he could probably run rings around her in terms of experience. But he wouldn't have any experience in being feckless and irresponsible, she reassured herself, so they were on equal ground there. With his father's ugly example to avoid, it was no wonder that he worshipped at the altar of self-discipline and conformity. 'And do you have any idea where you're going to find this haven of yuppiedom?'

'As a matter of fact I do. I'm going to live right in the middle of the action. I'm going to move into an apartment in one of those new, luxury, inner-city residential conversions . . . one with security and covered parking and a gym and a spa—maybe even a serviced apartment—'

'You set your sights high.' He interrupted her gleeful fantasising. 'Those places are extremely expensive to rent.'

Trust him to try to pin her down to earth with stuffy practicalities. 'Oh, I'm not going to rent. I'm going to buy,' she said airily.

He looked around the slightly shabby kitchen. 'That will take everything you get from this place, and probably more,' he estimated shrewdly.

She laughed in the face of his caution. 'So what? I have more. Plenty more, in fact. Thank goodness my father was very well insured.'

She didn't care if she sounded callous and mercenary. She intended to blow every cent of her inheritance: an apartment, a car, clothes, trips . . . her goal was the in-

stant gratification of every whim! What point was there
in scrimping and saving for years, as her parents had
done, if you might not be alive to enjoy the fruits of
your labours? In the last year of his life her father had
had enough money to take the world trip he had always
dreamed of, but his dreams had died with his wife.
Harriet was going to live hers before fate could snatch
them away.

'There can be ongoing costs involved with those
apartments—service fees and the slightly higher cost of
living,' Marcus was instructing her. 'You'll need to take
those into account and weigh them up against the pro-
jected capital appreciation of your investment—'

'I'm not making an investment,' Harriet interrupted.
'I just want somewhere fun to live for a while. Who
knows? I might feel like selling it again in another few
months and doing something else.'

'Like what?' he demanded with forbidding harshness.

'I don't know. Whatever I feel like at the time,' she
said impatiently. 'Life isn't a financial strategy, you
know. It doesn't have to be planned out to the minutest
detail in advance.'

'No, but it's wise to make some sort of provision for
contingencies. Long-term goals can provide you with a
sense of purpose and direction. If you don't have them
you run the risk of not recognising valuable opportunities when they present themselves, or uselessly frittering away what opportunities you *do* have—'

'Like the kettle is uselessly frittering away behind you,'
Harriet observed tartly. 'I guess people obsessed with
petty details rarely notice what's happening in the big
picture...'

He gave her a hard look as he switched off the kettle
and warmed the teapot, before measuring in the leaves
and adding the boiling water, his movements typically

precise and yet oddly ceremonial in their graceful ease of manner.

'You must drink a lot of tea,' she murmured.

'Probably more than I should,' he admitted. 'Morning and afternoon teas were my mother's speciality—the small rituals of a more gracious past. And since I don't drink alcohol I've become a connoisseur of the social substitute.'

He wouldn't find much to appreciate in her supermarket own-brand tea, thought Harriet wryly as she blurted out, 'Is that because of your father?'

He appeared unruffled by the personal question. 'Partly, I suppose... I'm afraid I might have a genetic predisposition to alcoholism. But mostly it's because I like to keep a clear head.'

'While all around you are losing theirs,' murmured Harriet. Didn't he realise how pointless it was, that there were some things that would always be beyond human control?

'Something like that. White or black?'

'White. But I forgot to buy any milk.'

He reached for the fridge door. 'I think I saw a carton left.' He took it out and frowned critically at the label. 'Non-fat? Surely you're not foolish enough to think you need to *diet*?'

He transferred his frown to her too slender figure and she could see that he was wondering whether she was suffering from an eating disorder.

'Of course not. I keep that for Frank—' Her heart began to pound and she clapped a hand over her stupid, runaway mouth.

'Frank?' He looked sharply at her, letting the fridge door drift shut. 'Who's Frank?'

She shook her head, putting her other hand over her mouth, desperately pressing the words back down her constricted throat, her eyes wide and blank with shock.

A lock of white hair fell forward over one dark eyebrow, catching in her stiffly mascaraed lashes and making her blink furiously.

His tone gentled. 'Harriet, who is Frank? A neighbour? Family?' When she shook her head wordlessly again, he stepped towards her. 'Then who? Obviously someone you know well.' His eyes narrowed on her white face and his voice hardened at her unconscious look of pleading, his anger edged with disbelief. 'Not your fiancé?'

'My fiancé?' Bewilderment mingled with her shock, the trembling words so muffled by her fingers that they were barely intelligible.

'*Ex*-fiancé, then. Has he come back?' She shook her head dumbly and backed up against the cabinets as he took another step closer. 'But you're still hoping he might, is that it? Why else would you still keep his preferred brand of milk in your fridge months after he walked out on you? Is that the reason behind your sudden desire to be a different woman—a last-ditch attempt to entice Frank back by distorting yourself into the kind of woman you think he finds exciting?'

A small sob of bitter laughter escaped her fingers and he wrenched them away, stripping her vulnerable mouth bare.

'Then answer me. Tell me *why*!'

'How typical of a male to think that there could only be one reason for a woman to want to change herself— to impress a man!' she choked. 'Let me go; you know nothing—*nothing*!' She tried to pull her wrists out of his hands but he held them grimly out to her sides.

'I know that he mauled you badly—'

She gasped. 'Keith was never violent!'' That had been part of the problem... his lack of passion. When their relationship had faltered under the continuing burden of her father's illness and it had seemed that Harriet would be caring for him well into the future, Keith hadn't even tried to fight for their love. He had simply given up.

'I meant emotionally—' He stopped and said with clipped intensity, 'Who in the hell is Keith?'

'My f—*ex*-fiancé.'

'Then who is Frank?'

'H-how did you know about my engagement?'

'The fact that you wore a diamond ring on your engagement finger was something of a clue,' he said drily.

She wouldn't have thought he would have noticed such an insignificant detail . . . particularly since the ring itself had been pretty insignificant—Keith wasn't given to extravagant gestures and what he'd saved on the tiny diamond chip had been carefully banked towards buying a house. 'I mean about Keith—about it breaking up?'

'You stopped wearing the ring,' he said, and just as she was relaxing at the thought that, naturally, he was above listening to office gossip he added cruelly, 'And I believe you mentioned it to several people at the office on New Year's Eve.'

Her white face flooded with colour and she went limp in his hold. 'Oh, no! You mean at the party, when I, when I . . . ?'

'Was somewhat inebriated, yes. Oh, don't worry . . . your ramblings were quite circumspect . . . no names, no intimate secrets revealed, just sad references to the man who let you down when you most needed him and how you couldn't hurt him as much as he hurt you because he obviously didn't care enough to *be* hurt.'

'Oh, God . . .' She couldn't hide her face in her hands, so she lifted her chin and confronted him proudly. Thank goodness she had no coherent memories of that wretched party! No wonder everyone had been so discreetly kind the next day. She squared her slender shoulders. 'Do you really think that I'd want a man like *that* back gain?'

'Women scorned do strange things.'

'I wasn't *scorned*. As it happened *I* was the one who broke it off,' she flung at him.

'Were you?'

'Yes. He gave me an ultimatum and I rejected the choice that included him.' Keith had been afraid that the financial and emotional cost of providing long-term care for her ailing father would be too great a drain on their marriage, but the idea of placing someone she loved in an institution, no matter how well run, was abhorrent to Harriet. It was ironic that her father had died only weeks after she had given Keith his modest ring back.

'Go to bed with me or the wedding's off?'

Her eyes burned with fury. 'Of course not! We were already—'

She sucked in her breath as she realised what he'd goaded her into betraying.

'Lovers,' he finished for her, with a gentleness that was at odds with the inflexible grip on her wrists. 'Relax, Harriet; there's no shame in saying it. Nor any sin in an adult woman committing herself heart, mind and body to the man with whom she believes she is going to spend the rest of her life.'

'Then why do I feel as if I'm being crucified for it?' she said pointedly, tugging once more against his captive hold.

'Because you're still evading the original question. Who is Frank?'

He had the tenacity of a bulldog...or was just someone who was very focused on achieving his aims.

'Why do you have to know?' she said huskily. Her eyes stung. What was it about Marcus Fox that lured her into thinking he would understand? Even she recognised that her reactions had been way out of proportion to the event.

'Because the mere thought of him took all the light out of your eyes. What has he done to you, Harriet?'

'Nothing.' She looked up at him with deeply wounded eyes. 'I—he's dead. Frank's dead.' She had to repeat it twice to make it seem real. 'He was killed...last week. He—I came home from work on Friday night and found him...' Her voice sank to a whisper and she closed her eyes, her lashes wet.

'Found him where? Here in the house?'

'No.' She sniffed inelegantly, opening her eyes as she said brokenly, 'Outside, at the side of the road—in—in the gutter.'

'The *gutter*?' He dropped her hands and took her shoulders in a powerful grip. His usual poker-face was vivid with stunned emotion. The knowledge of his shared outrage made the tears tremble on her lashes. She hadn't cried when it happened. She had been too angry, too betrayed by the sheer unfairness of life. Something in her had snapped, had driven her to cry, Enough!

'I think it was a hit-and-run. He was just left there...like a piece of rubbish...'

'My God, what did the police say?' he said roughly.

'I didn't call them. What was the point? What could they do? What could anyone do?' She smeared the tears away with the back of her hand. 'So...I...buried him myself...in the back garden, by the roses.'

He recoiled without loosening his grip. *'You buried a man in your back garden?'*

She peered at him through her blurry eyes, astonished. 'What man?'

'Frank!'

Realisation hit her like an avalanche. 'Frank wasn't a *man*,' she cried shrilly. 'He was my cat.'

'Your *cat*?' If she hadn't been so upset she might have found his expression of confused relief funny. Not many people got to confuse that razor-sharp brain. 'My God, Frank is a *cat*?'

'Was, not is.' Harriet was stricken by a sudden mental image of a furry ginger face and sleepy copper eyes and the comforting purr that was always there when she woke in the night, reminding her that she was not entirely alone in the world. Her throat thickened again, forming a dam against the renewed pressure of tears as she braced herself to be told sternly that she was overreacting.

'I know a cat isn't as important as a person,' she whispered, 'but animals feel pain too... He was old, and a bit slow. I should have shut him inside when I went to work, but it gets stuffy in the house sometimes and he loves—loved to stroll and sleep in the garden. He used to curl up by the roses, where I buried him...' The dam broke, her grief rushing down the spillway. She hiccuped and stuffed a fist in her mouth to try to stem the salty tide.

'Oh, *Harriet*!' Suddenly she was snatched hard against his chest and his strong arms were wrapped around her, blissfully, suffocatingly, painfully tight, supporting her, rocking her, pressing her wet cheek against the satin lapel of his jacket as she struggled not to make a complete idiot of herself. 'Don't!' he said as she choked and gulped. 'Don't fight it, Harriet. Cry if you want to...'

'But I don't want to,' she sobbed. 'It's silly to be so upset. He was only a cat!' They were all the things she had expected him to say.

'But he was yours...' He hesitated as he made a leap of perception. 'Or was he your parents'?'

Her hand fisted against his chest. Clever, clever man. 'No, but they gave him to me as a birthday present when I was eight years old. A marmalade kitten, because I loved marmalade. It...it was a family joke.' Only now there was no family...no one to share the silly joke with...

'My goodness, he was a venerable age, then,' he murmured gently.

'He was eighteen,' she sobbed. 'And don't tell me that he had a good long life—as if it makes it somehow easier to lose him ... It *doesn't*, it makes it *harder*!'

'I know. I know.' The vibrating growl of his voice in her ear where it was pressed against his chest was not unlike Frank's deep, rumbling purr. 'Of course it hurts. You've known him most of your life. He was a link to your childhood ...'

Shattered by compassion and understanding where she had expected derision and an admonition to pull herself together, Harriet felt her brave new image totter and collapse. Escaping into boundless grief, she burrowed past his jacket to the snowy-white shirt-front, which soaked up her hot tears until the wet silk was transparent under her cheek.

She hardly noticed when he picked her up and carried her across the small dining room to the deeply padded window-seat, where he settled her on his substantial lap. He patted her shuddering back and nudged the tumbled curls away from her sticky forehead with the roughness of his jaw, and all the while held her so tightly that she knew she was safe, that she wouldn't fall into the yawning pit of emptiness that lurked at the edge of her consciousness. The luxury of a simple hug was infinitely seductive, and Harriet cried all the harder in the knowledge that when Marcus took his arms away she would again be devastatingly alone.

But he didn't take them away, and when at last her crying jag was over and she lay quiet against his chest Harriet became aware that it wasn't an impassive rock beneath her, but a living, breathing man of flesh and sinew and pumping blood. Her arms had wound themselves around his waist underneath his splayed jacket, and she could feel the slow, deep expansion and contraction of his ribcage through the thinness of his shirt. Her breast was compressed over his heart and the rhythmic thudding against her soft tissue created streamers of sensation that radiated out to lace her body with the knowledge of his powerful life force.

She couldn't see his face but his lower jaw rested on her head, trapping it against his shoulder, and she could feel him swallow with the whole of her scalp—little ripples of motion along his throat that massaged her ultra-sensitive skin and made the blood rush to her head. If she looked up at him her mouth would touch the dark, grainy skin under his chin, and if she parted her lips she might taste the fine whiskers which had abraded her temples with the delicate roughness of a cat's tongue.

His scent was heavy, musky, unmasked by any hint of the cologne she thought she had detected at the nightclub. Now he merely smelled of Marcus—mellow and rich and memorable, like the aroma of a fine cigar. His strong thighs were warm and relaxed beneath hers, slightly splayed to cup her slender bottom, tilting her body so that her hip was tucked against the apex of his legs where the soft cushion of his masculinity informed her that, while she might be prickling all over with physical awareness, his embrace was solely one of consolation.

Feeling safe and yet aware of a tantalising danger, Harriet inhaled and let out a shuddering sigh and wriggled deeper into his lap. The malleable outline against her hip was large, and Harriet felt another wave of prickly heat wash over her as she indulged her sinful curiosity and wondered what it would take to arouse a man of his iron self-control and how different he would feel in his state of excitement.

She imagined what would happen if she was lying like this in his arms but for some inexplicable but necessary reason they were both completely nude. Surely he wouldn't be unaffected then, no matter how skinny or pathetic he thought she was? He was a man and he wouldn't be able to help himself. He might fight against his primitive instincts because he didn't want to hurt her, but he would eventually succumb to the feel of her naked breasts and thighs rubbing against him. He would kiss her fiercely, and smother her small breasts in his big, clever hands, and then he would go thick and hard against her squirming bottom and he would turn her in his lap and—

With a squeak of horror Harriet jerked upright, appalled at the trend of her fantasising. Marcus lifted his head, loosening his grip instantly, and she scooted towards his knees, looking back at him as if he were the devil, her lips parting in dismay as her gaze fell onto the large wet patch her tears had left on his shirt, faintly streaked with specks of her waterproof mascara. It looked stunningly indecent, she thought faintly, as if she had been nuzzling and drooling over him . . . which she virtually had been!

'Feeling better?'

'Y-yes, thank you.'

She blushed to the core of her being, feeling as if she had violated his trust. He had offered her kind consolation and she had responded by conducting a mental rape. But then, the only way a woman *could* take a man of honour against his will was in her imagination. Why, if she were truly depraved, she could force the cool, proud, forbiddingly severe Marcus Fox to be her lover over and over in her dreams and he would be powerless to stop her. She could do anything she liked to and with him and no one would be any the wiser. Harriet crammed the forbidden thought back into the wicked corner in her mind whence it had sprung.

How shocked he would be if he knew what she had been thinking! She felt even worse when, brushing away her babbling apologies for the damage to his shirt, he produced a white silk square from his breast pocket and gravely wiped her tear-stained cheeks. Then, his hands almost spanning her waist, he gently set her back on her feet and suggested that the tea must definitely be drawn by now.

Actually it was almost cold, but he politely pretended not to notice and sipped it quietly at the kitchen table, allowing Harriet to flutter on about nothing in particular until she had recovered her equilibrium.

When she had, he immediately upset it again by saying quietly, as she carried the empty cups back to the bench, 'If you're worried about being alone tonight, perhaps you'd like me to stay?'

Spend the night with Marcus Fox? Fastidious Marcus Fox showering in her old-fashioned bathroom, soaping himself with her scented soap, drying his lean, hard body on one of her towels? Marcus Fox sleeping in her spare bed? Marcus awake in *her* bed...big and bare, arms folded behind his head, revealing the thick, dark tufts of silky-soft hair under his arms, his slitted eyes watching Harriet play the slave girl, dancing around him, shedding her glittering gold metal skin inch by tantalising inch until he erupted out of his gentlemanly skin—?

'*No!*' The cups crashed into the sink and she spun around, quickly pinning on a bright smile as she met his eyes, slitted just as they had been in her fantasy, but not with desire, just with his infernal, impersonal kindness. Having witnessed her breakdown, he was concerned for her well-being, that was all. 'I mean no, thank you. That won't be necessary. It was just a delayed reaction, that's all. I'm fine now.'

'If you're sure,' he said slowly.

'Very sure,' she declared.

'Well, perhaps it's time I let you go to bed...'

Past time, thought Harriet fervently, if her hot flushes at his every innocent comment were anything to go by. She was furious at the trick her body had played on her mind. Marcus Fox had made it very clear that he was sexually immune to blondes. She had no wish to waste any more of her life on futile hopes. An unrequited desire was definitely not on the agenda!

'Uh—about tomorrow...?' she said as she followed him to the door.

He halted on the threshold. 'Yes?'

'I—do you still want me to work with Nicola?'

'Why wouldn't I?'

She shrugged. 'Well, I just thought—having seen how unstable I am—that it might have put you off... You can change your mind, you know; I won't be offended...'

He tipped up her chin with his crooked forefinger and pressed his thumb warningly over her full lips. 'You don't know me very well yet, do you, Harriet? When I make a commitment I stand by it. When I make a promise I keep it. And when I make up my mind about something it takes more fire-power than you pack in that sweet little body of yours to change it.

'I'll stand outside until I've heard you bolt your door. I won't leave until I know you're safe. Sleep tight, blondie.'

He removed his thumb from her tingling lips and replaced it with a single, brief salute of his mouth. Then he did precisely as he had promised.

CHAPTER SIX

'So, NICOLA—what do you think of these?'

Harriet held up the chunky earrings to her ears, jangling them so that they brushed against the shoulder-straps of her emerald-green, sleeveless linen shift.

Nicola Fox looked at her, the gravity of expression in her green eyes very reminiscent of her father's at his most restrained.

'They're very nice,' she said politely.

'Oh, come off it, Nicola—what do you *really* think?' Harriet demanded impatiently.

After two and a half days in the girl's company she had learned that the only way to break through that polite wall of reserve was to bulldoze brutally over it. Far from being the bored, restless, sulky little rich girl that Harriet had been prepared to suffer, Marcus Fox's daughter had proved to be a quiet, respectful, well-brought-up young lady with a penchant for taking life too seriously. In short, she reminded Harriet uncomfortably of herself at the same age!

'Well, they are a little garish,' Nicola conceded, studying the fake-gold and green glass earrings.

'They are, aren't they?' Harriet grinned. 'They match this dress perfectly. I'll take them,' she told the salesgirl.

She heard the small sigh at her side. 'They look quite heavy. You won't be able to wear them until your ears heal properly.'

She certainly was her father's daughter, seeing problems before they existed. It was Harriet's turn to sigh. Then she brightened determinedly. She had vowed not to let anything or anyone clip her wings. Besides, who better to show Nicola what she was missing by being such a goody-two-shoes? 'Hey, why don't you get your ears pierced too, while we're here?'

'Uh, no, I don't think so, thank you.'

Harriet pounced on the faint trace of wistfulness she detected. 'Why not? Lots of girls much younger than you have their ears pierced. It's very in.'

'I don't think Granny would like it. And my school doesn't allow you to wear jewellery—'

'Mrs Jerome's two generations removed from you; naturally you're going to have different tastes. As for school, you have two weeks before you go back—by then you'll be able to take the sleepers out during the day,' she pointed out. 'And if you decide you don't like the look or it creates too much of a fuss, you can always let them grow over...'

'My mother had pierced ears,' said Nicola suddenly, looking at the classier selection under the glass case of the shop counter. 'She had tons of earrings. Daddy keeps all her jewellery for me in his safe.'

'Well, there you are, then—it's destiny!'

'Maybe I should ask Daddy first...'

'I think you're quite old enough to make decisions like this for yourself,' said Harriet traitorously. 'They're your ears, after all, not his.'

Nicola giggled, sounding like a careless teenager for the first time in Harriet's presence. 'He'd look pretty silly in earrings.'

'Oh, I don't know.' Harriet pretended to consider the matter seriously. 'It depends what kind. A gold ring in one ear and a stud through his nose might liven the old man up... or do I mean a stud in his ear and a ring through his nose?' she said drily.

Nicola's quick mind picked up the reference. 'Nobody tells Daddy what to do.'

The mixture of awe and pride was telling. She had a bad case of parent-worship, Harriet decided sourly. 'Don't you believe it, honey. He just likes you to *think* he's omnipotent. It's women who really run the world. Miss Broadbent, for example. She tells him what to do all the time!'

'Only because she organises his diary.'

'Ah, that's what *he* thinks... he doesn't even realise he's just a puppet chairman—the poor, helpless pawn of a cunning woman!'

They both laughed in unison at this far-fetched notion of Marcus Fox at anyone's mercy, then Nicola stopped and said uncertainly, 'You don't really think Daddy's an old man, do you?'

'Well, he's not exactly young any more,' said Harriet flippantly. Then she saw the sober, unblinking green gaze, magnified by the owlish glasses, and worried that her determination to reject any reminder of Marcus Fox as a virile, desirable male might be stoking Nicola's hidden fears about her father's mortality. 'But he's certainly not old,' she said, relenting. 'And he's obviously very fit and energetic—'

'Yes, he is, isn't he?' Nicola was eager to add, 'He needs very little sleep, you see—only four or five hours every night. He said it used to drive Mummy crazy!'

'Really,' said Harriet faintly as she absently paid for her earrings, thinking that it would certainly drive her crazy to wake up to Marcus Fox prowling around in the dark, looking for a way to work off some of his excess energy. And he was like that every night? It must have made for a very active marriage...

'Yes, he says that's why he's such a high achiever—because of all those extra hours when there was nothing else to do but read or work!'

'Really,' murmured Harriet again, pinkening. But of course Marcus Fox would only tell his daughter the innocuous stuff!

'Oh, look at those, Nicola.' She tapped the glass over a pair of pearl studs to distract herself from wicked thoughts. 'They'd look perfect on you and you can't say they're too garish. Come on; why don't you get it done? It doesn't hurt ... that is, only for a second or two.'

'Well ...'

It took a little more persuasion, but ten minutes later they strolled back out onto the busy city pavement, self-consciously sporting matching gold sleepers. Knowledge of her own daring had brought a flush of colour to Nicola's pale, composed features and her eyes were sparkling. Harriet felt a guilty pang at the sight of her subdued delight, aware that her own motives in encouraging the girl to do something that went against her cautious nature were scarcely altruistic.

'Where shall we go now?' she said, ruthlessly ignoring her niggling conscience.

Nicola looked at the small gold watch on her wrist. 'We only have seventeen minutes left,' she calculated. 'Perhaps we'd better start heading back to the office.' She adjusted her spectacles as she added tentatively, 'We haven't had anything to eat yet either.'

'Shopping is much more important than eating,' said Harriet, grinning in satisfaction at the clutch of paper carrier bags they were both carrying. 'We can pick up some sandwiches to have at our desks.' A late-model car pulled into the kerb inches from their toes and inspiration came to her in a flash. 'I know! Let's go back to the car.'

'Why, where are we going?' asked Nicola, trotting at her heels like an anxious puppy. 'More shopping? It won't take long, will it?'

Harriet laughed as she strode along the pavement, aware of the male attention that she was attracting with her dazzling hair and bright dress and the over-large dark glasses which masked her face and made people wonder whether she was a celebrity in disguise. 'No, it won't take long. I know *exactly* what I want and where to buy it!'

It didn't come in green, to match her dress, so she had to settle for white, which, as the salesman pointed out, choking slightly on the words, would go with everything in her wardrobe.

Harriet was still laughing over his shock as they swooped into the entrance of the underground car park used by Trident employees, Nicola clutching the dashboard on the Porsche as if she expected to be hurtled through the windscreen at any moment.

'Relax; I've never had an accident in ten years of driving,' Harriet said, thrilling to the power that throbbed under her control. The Carrera was a new cabriolet, and the wild ride with the soft top folded down had whipped her hair into a frenzy that matched her spirits.

'Yes, but I bet you've never driven a Porsche before,' Nicola gasped.

Harriet laughed again. 'I did bunny-hop a bit, didn't I, when we started off? Did you see the salesman's face when I said I wanted to trade in my Mazda?' The car had been her mother's, lovingly cared for but undeniably old.

'He thought you were just kidding until you brought out your cheque-book,' recalled Nicola, relaxing slightly now that they were out of the dense traffic. 'And then you asked if there was a discount for cash and he nearly fell over himself to give it to you!'

'It just goes to prove the saying "who dares wins"!' Harriet said smugly, aware that her former self would never have dreamed of wasting so much money on a car, or have had the temerity to demand that a haughty salesman knock a few thousand dollars off the price.

The Porsche's tyres squealed satisfyingly as she went down the ramp which opened out into Trident's reserved parking spaces. She glanced in her rear-view mirror as she cut smartly in front of a car filtering sedately in from another entrance. In the next instant she spied a small white sign above a yawning parking space. Obeying a sense of sheer devilry, she pulled into it and cut the engine.

'You can't park here,' squeaked Nicola, pointing to the stern warning that said 'CHAIRMAN'.

'I just have.' Harriet ignored the impatient blast of a horn and hopped out of the car, leaning over to re-arrange the carrier bags that she had crammed behind her seat. 'Come on; we don't want to be any later than we already are.'

'But—' Nicola's protest was drowned out by another toot and a terse male voice taking up her cause.

'Excuse me, but would you mind moving your car? That space is reserved, as you can see from the sign directly in front of you.'

Harriet turned and smiled brilliantly at the irritated driver leaning on the open window of his dark green Volvo. 'Is it? Oh, dear, silly me. Still, first in, first served, I always say.'

The expression on Marcus Fox's face was priceless. 'Harriet?' His momentary disbelief was eclipsed by a dark frown as he watched her lean a slender hip against the dashing white car. 'Where did that thing come from?' he rapped out.

Harriet removed her dark glasses and dangled them carelessly from a manicured finger. 'The Porsche fairy left it under my pillow. Aren't I lucky—?'

'We bought it, Daddy,' interrupted Nicola, scrambling out of her seat and hurrying around the rear bumper. 'Just now...at least, Harriet did. Isn't it beautiful? It's brand-new.'

'I can see that,' he grated. Ignoring the fact that his car was blocking the narrow lane between the parked cars, he thrust open his door and got out, striding over to stand beside Harriet, hands on hips as he surveyed her flashy acquisition with deep disapproval. 'This vehicle is way too over-powered for your needs—'

'Hmm, sounds like a bad case of Porsche-envy to me, Marcus,' she murmured provocatively, and he gave her a crushing look.

'I don't happen to subscribe to the myth that a car is a sexual metaphor. If I cared to own one of these I would; however, I happen to think that it's an exercise in point-lessness having so much horsepower lying idle under the bonnet when the maximum speed limit around town is fifty kilometres an hour—'

'Harriet went a bit faster than that, though, didn't you, Harriet? She almost got a speeding ticket, but the policeman who stopped us was very nice; he let her off with a warning.'

Harriet had time to wish that Nicola were a little less honest in her excitement as Marcus's head went up with a jerk, his deep voice echoing around the concrete walls.

'She *what*?'

If the roof to the car park had been any lower he would have hit it literally, as well as figuratively.

'I just let it surge a little bit at the wrong moment,' she admitted. 'The officer was very understanding when I explained that I was still getting used to the gears.'

'I'll bet he was,' growled Marcus out of the stern corner of his mouth, his eyes flicking over her bare arms and legs. 'He must have wondered who was more out of control—you or the Porsche.'

'At no time were we in any danger,' Harriet responded hotly. 'You know I wouldn't have driven carelessly with Nicola in the car.'

'Not even to show off a little?'

She bristled with disdain. 'When you drive a Porsche you don't *have* to show off. That's the whole point of owning one.'

He surprised her with a bark of genuine laughter. 'True. And yes, I do know that, however reckless you might seem, your conscience would never let you put anyone else's life at risk.'

She was sure that there was something in the comment that she should object to but as she turned it over in her mind he asked, 'So how much did you pay for this showy little piece?'

'None of your business,' said Harriet, at the same moment as Nicola piped up with the answer.

The black eyebrows shot up and Harriet smirked. 'Got a good deal, didn't I?'

'If you'd told me you were on the market for a new car, I could have negotiated one more cheaply through the dealer who handles our fleet cars.'

This time it was her blood pressure which shot up. 'I wasn't "on the market",' she said. 'I just bought it on impulse.'

'On impulse,' he repeated.

'Yes.' She flashed him her teeth. 'You do know what that is, don't you, Marcus? An action that's not tiresomely planned and/or had all the fun negotiated out of it!'

'Yes, I do know what an impulse is. It's stealing the chairman's reserved car-park space out from under his nose. Move it, Harriet, or I'll call the building supervisor and have it towed away.'

Genuinely shocked, Harriet spread her hands protectively over her car's gleaming paintwork. 'You wouldn't! Not a *Porsche*!'

'A Porsche is just another car as far as I'm concerned. And do you remember what I told you, Harriet,' he added silkily, 'about issuing dares?'

She remembered everything about that night. Harriet tried to look unconcerned. 'All right; it was only a joke anyway. I knew it was your car behind me.'

'I did manage to figure that out,' he said drily, and turned to his daughter. 'What made you decide to eat extra early today? I was surprised to go down to Filing and find you'd both already gone. I was going to take you out to lunch.'

Nicola's small face registered her disappointment. 'I didn't know. But...you took us out yesterday and Harriet said there was no way you'd be free two days in a row...'

'Did she indeed?' The cool blue eyes looked amused, as if he knew that the sole reason why she had decided they would take an early lunch-break was to avoid just such a recurrence.

Harriet lifted her chin. 'You told me yourself that your lunchtimes were fully booked up for the next couple of weeks, so naturally I didn't think that it was even a remote possibility.'

'My schedule has undergone some rearrangement since then,' he said smoothly. 'I find myself with some unexpected free time.'

Harriet felt a flutter of panic. 'What a pity our lunch-hour is over, then,' she oozed sweetly. 'I know what a stickler you are for timekeeping and not wanting Nicola to receive any special treatment just because she's your daughter. I'll just shift my car and we'll be on our way back to the office.'

She took the unsmiling inclination of his head as an indication of acceptance and hurried to carry out her task, wincing as she clashed the gears under his critical stare.

By the time she had manoeuvred into one of the unmarked empty spaces and carefully locked the car, Marcus had parked the Volvo and was standing talking with his daughter. As she approached they both turned.

'Nicola tells me that you were so busy shopping, you didn't get time to eat.'

'No... well, we're going to send out for some sandwiches from the office,' said Harriet, casting a reproachful look at the girl. But she couldn't really blame Nicola. Apart from having first call on her loyalty, Marcus Fox was an expert in worming things out of people!

'I have a better idea. I haven't eaten yet either, so why don't we have a quick lunch together now and make up the extra time by working a little longer this evening? Deal?'

She might have known that any deal-making didn't include her, brooded Harriet darkly a bare ten minutes later as she perused a large menu.

Like father like daughter, she thought, frowning over the top of her menu at the pair ranged against her on the other side of the small, elegantly set table.

Nicola might be shy and retiring, but she possessed a strong will and, having got what she wanted—lunch with her father—she had blossomed into a delightful chatterbox. From little things she had said over the past couple of days, Harriet was beginning to suspect that Nicola didn't *not* want to go to school so much as she wanted to spend more time with her busy father... and the only way to do that was to invade the separate world of his workplace. Escaping her daunting grandmother's rigid supervision also probably had something to do with her sudden desire for a job, and she was clever enough to have realised that the most logical thing for her highly

protective father to do when faced with such a request
was to tuck her safely away under his corporate care.

Oh, yes, in her own quiet way Nicola Fox was as adept
at manipulating events to her advantage as was her
father. It was probably genetic! When Marcus had said
that his daughter was mature for her age Harriet had
mistakenly jumped to the conclusion that he had been
referring to her over-eagerness for social and sexual de-
velopment. Instead he had been warning her to expect
a mini-adult. Harriet would have to pull her socks up if
she was going to avoid being further entangled in their
family intrigues. She was supposed to be a queen on the
chessboard of life, not a sacrificial pawn.

'Hungry?' asked Marcus, looking up from his menu
to catch Harriet's muted glare.

She lowered the menu to show him her teeth.
'Ravenous!'

'Good. You look as if a puff of wind would blow you
over. Soup to start with, and then something more substantial, don't you think?'

'Mmm, I'm starving!' said Nicola, triggering a pang
of guilt in Harriet at her thoughtlessness in brushing aside
the younger girl's comments about finding something to
eat during their shopping spree.

'It's too hot for soup,' she announced contrarily,
having been eyeing the description of the mouth-watering
soup of the day. She rapidly skimmed down the prices,
seeking the most expensive items on a very expensive
menu.

She had to pay him back somehow for contriving to
torture her with his company! At the restaurant that he
had whisked them off to yesterday, Harriet had been too
embarrassed by the memory of herself crying in his lap
to do anything but pick at the omelette that she had
distractedly ordered. Marcus had been infuriatingly relaxed and natural, refusing to leave her out of the con-

versation, so that, for Nicola's sake, she had had to talk and smile and act as if she were perfectly comfortable lunching with the chairman of the board.

It had been the first time that she had spoken with him since he had kissed her on her doorstep, and Harriet had had great difficulty in keeping her eyes away from his mouth, suddenly seeing sensuality where before she had noticed only sternness. Marcus had claimed that he had wanted to allow Nicola a full day to settle in before he formally celebrated her new job by squiring her to lunch, but Harriet had wondered whether he had waited to be sure that she wasn't going to presume too much on a casual kiss now regretted. As if she would! The modern, free-thinking woman dispensed such favours like candy.

She glowered at the menu. So what if his kiss had been the equivalent of Belgian chocolate on the candy-scale? That was merely because so far she only had boiled sweets with which to compare it. She wasn't going to let one disastrous evening put her off. Yesterday she had allowed him to tie her into knots worrying about what he was thinking and what he thought *she* was thinking. Today she didn't care!

'Harriet?' She looked up to find the waiter standing patiently beside her, as he had obviously been for some time. Marcus leaned across to run a kind finger along the top of her menu. 'Would you like me to explain anything for you?'

Now he was implying that she was too unsophisticated to understand restaurant French. It was about time he forgot her pathetic performance of the other night and learned to respect her toughness!

'Yes,' she said crisply. 'You can explain why men complain about the talkativeness of women but insist on interpreting their thoughtful silences as helpless confusion.' Harriet snapped her menu closed and reeled off her exorbitant choices, her eyes directly challenging his.

She was immensely gratified when he was the first to look away. His lids fell, his long black lashes concealing his expression as he looked down at his menu. A tiny compression of his mouth a few seconds later was the only hint that he realised what she had done.

'Wow! Are you really going to eat all that?' said Nicola, impressed, as she gave the waiter her small order with a shy smile.

'Of course she is,' commented Marcus, neatly cutting off any thought of a dignified retreat. 'Harriet is a woman governed by her appetites. Just the soup of the day and the grilled fish, thank you, Sean.' He handed the menu back without taking his eyes off Harriet's flushed face. 'Isn't that right, Harriet?'

'The soup and the fish?' She deliberately misunderstood. 'You'd know that better than I, since you obviously come here often.'

'What makes you say that?'

'You called the waiter by name.'

'He was wearing a name-tag,' said Marcus blandly. 'Didn't you notice?'

No. Of course she hadn't! Marcus Fox had a habit of narrowing down her range of focus to a dangerous extent. She made great play of looking around her now, pretending an interest in the other diners that she didn't feel. Several men caught her eye and she gave them each the bold hint of a smile and immediately felt better. She picked up the wine list that Marcus was ignoring and leafed idly through it.

'I know something that *you* haven't noticed,' she heard Nicola say.

'Oh, and what's that?' Her father instantly turned all his attention to her. 'That you've spent your first paycheque before you've even earned it? How like a woman!'

Harriet winced, but Nicola didn't seem to mind his rampant sexism. Perhaps she thought he wasn't serious, but Harriet detected the inherent cynicism in the teasing remark. 'I hardly bought anything. It was Harriet who was doing all the shopping. She bought tons of new clothes...she even offered to buy some for me but they weren't really things that I would wear.'

'Poor Harriet. Is my daughter proving difficult to corrupt?' Marcus transferred his teasing to her.

She smiled thinly at him as Nicola laughed. 'Come on, Daddy, there's something different about me from this morning.' She turned her head from side to side suggestively.

Through her lowered lashes Harriet watched in malicious enjoyment as Marcus's shoulders tensed and his teasing expression stilled. 'You've had your ears pierced.'

Nicola ignored the slight reverberation of shock in his voice. 'Yes; do you like it?' she said eagerly.

There was an anxious moment and then Harriet saw his shoulders relax. 'Very chic, darling. I'm glad you prefer the elegant look to the punk appeal of a stud through the nose!'

Nicola looked at Harriet and giggled at the memory of their earlier exchange.

Marcus noticed the glances. 'Was this pre or *après* Porsche?' he asked drily.

'Oh, before,' said Nicola, looking suddenly uneasy as she sensed the dichotomy in his attitude. She fiddled with her napkin. 'You really don't mind, then, Daddy?'

He covered her hand with his, squeezing it gently. 'I do, actually, but only because it's made me realise that my little girl is even more grown-up than I realised...you don't come rushing to me with every bump and scrape any more and you have rights to privacy and independence that exclude me. I'm just being selfish, I suppose... but I'm glad that you still respect my judgement enough to ask for my opinion—even if it's after the fact!'

'I did think I ought to ask you first,' Nicola allowed generously, 'but Harriet said I was old enough to make my own decision.'

'Did she indeed?' he murmured, removing his hand and contemplating Harriet's guilty face.

'Well, she is,' Harriet defended herself.

'Oh, I agree. Didn't I just say that?' he asked with a mildness that sent nervous shivers down her spine. Surely he would now want to reassess her position of influence over his daughter?

'I thought it might hurt, but Harriet hadn't flinched at all,' continued Nicola blithely, 'so I knew it must be OK, because she said she's a coward about pain...'

Something flared in the blue eyes as Marcus suddenly reached across the table and thrust his fingers into the wavy blonde mass brushing Harriet's cheek, combing it back to expose her ear with its small, shining stud.

'Well, well, well; so you've had your ears pierced too,' he said huskily, tucking the curls behind the curve of her ear so that he could study the full effect, the tips of his fingers brushing against the little strip of sensitive skin there, causing a small, electric buzz in her hearing. 'What a tempting example of your daring to set before an impressionable teenager.'

It struck her that he was using his curiosity as an excuse to touch her, to deliberately cross some hidden boundary of acceptable public behaviour, but before she could move out of his reach his thumb slid forward and stroked the soft pink lobe, and she jumped. 'Sore?'

He was mocking her. He knew that wasn't the reason for her sensitivity. 'Just a little bit tender,' she said, tilting her head so that his only polite choice was to let his hand fall back to the table.

'Like your conscience?' he murmured, hitting the nail on the head with his usual annoying precision as their first course arrived. 'I suppose I should consider myself lucky you didn't come back with matching Porsches as well!'

'I haven't learnt to drive yet,' Nicola reminded him, digging into her salad. 'Some of my friends got their licences as soon as they were fifteen—'

Marcus shuddered and sternly cut in, 'Harriet is *not*, I repeat *not* going to teach you to drive in her Porsche. And you are *not* to even think of asking her.'

'But *you* will, won't you, Daddy?' Nicola said confidently. 'Then I wouldn't have to ask Granny to take me everywhere when you're away.'

'You needn't think that a driving licence automatically comes with your own car,' Marcus warned over a spoonful of fragrant soup, 'because you'll have to have at least a year's experience on the road before I'll even consider buying you one. I'm willing to start you off but I think a driving school is the best place to learn to cope with today's traffic—and then a defensive driving course.'

'Who taught you to drive, Harriet?' asked Nicola, obviously seeking an ally.

Harriet, who had never tasted caviare before, was discovering that she hated it. As soon as she got home she was going to toss out the unopened jars from her fridge, since there was no longer any Frank to dine on her scraps.

'My father was too impatient and my mother too terrified, so my elder brother, Tim, ended up teaching me,' she said, putting off the evil moment when she would have to pass another fishy, squelchy mouthful across her shrinking taste buds.

'I didn't know you had a brother,' said Marcus, his eyes bright blue with curiosity, and Harriet knew that she couldn't stomach another mouthful.

'That was delicious,' she lied, pushing the rest of the caviare out of her olfactory range.

'I think caviare's revolting,' said Nicola frankly, wrinkling her nose. 'Granny had it at one of her cocktail parties. I don't know how you can bear to eat it.'

'Actually she didn't,' Marcus pointed out with a straight face, but with eyes that were mocking.

'I only wanted a taste,' said Harriet airily.

'Are you going to *only taste* everything else you ordered too?' asked Marcus wryly.

She shrugged. 'I don't know. I live from moment to moment.' At least she had got him off the subject of Tim.

Fortunately for her stomach, for she had discovered that her flippant claim to being ravenous was actually fact, her main course was divine, and she fell on it with dainty greed, closing her eyes in blissful gratitude as her first bite of venison melted on her tongue, releasing a tantalising burst of flavour from the exotic stuffing and cunningly blended medley of sauces. When she opened her eyes it was to see Marcus, fork arrested in the air as he watched her embrace the glory of the food with her whole being.

'Good?'

It was so much so that she couldn't resent his amusement.

'Fabulous!' she sighed. In the past year she had been in danger of forgetting that food could be more than merely fuel for the body, it could be an inspiration to the senses!

'Well, perhaps this is a good time to suggest that it might be an excellent idea to have someone give you a few lessons on the correct handling of a high-performance vehicle, so you don't attract the attention of any more friendly policemen.'

Harriet almost choked on a piece of meat. She coughed into her napkin and stared at him suspiciously over the starched white folds. 'Like who, for instance?'

'Well, I've owned a sports car or two myself, in my distant, salad days...when I had more testosterone than sense. I think I could provide you with some valuable advice.'

The idea of being trapped in the intimate confines of her sexy new car with Marcus Fox critically observing her every reaction to the traffic—and to him—gave her the shivers.

'Thank you, but I don't think—'

'I think you should, Harriet,' Nicola interrupted quietly. 'The man who killed my mother was driving a rental car, and Granny told me that the police said he put it into the wrong gear when he was trying to avoid a collision and that's why he swerved into Mummy's car.'

'Oh, I didn't know,' said Harriet, her antagonism abruptly subdued.

'Daddy's good at explaining things and he's really patient. He won't shout at you if you do something wrong.'

'Consider it a small favour in exchange for a large lunch,' he said blandly. 'Shall we say you'll take me for a small spin after work this evening?' His mouth quirked. 'Not literally, of course...'

'I'm sorry, I'm busy this evening,' Harriet was pleased to be able to tell him truthfully. 'I'll have to rush home to get ready as it is.'

'Nightclubbing again?' he asked sardonically.

'No, I have a lesson in Thai cooking.'

'Fair enough. Tomorrow evening, then.'

'Tomorrow is Saturday,' she pointed out.

'All the better.'

'Not for me. I'm going to be away all weekend,' she said cheerfully.

His cool look became alert. 'Away where?'

'The tramping club I've joined. We're going down to Coromandel to tramp a national-park trail. We won't be back until late Sunday night.'

He frowned. 'Monday, then.'

She had to think. 'French For Beginners.'

'*Tuesday*?'

Ah, that one she didn't have to think about. 'On Tuesday I have a date.'

'With whom?' he queried politely.

She shrugged. 'No one you would know.'

'Try me.'

She sighed. 'His name is Greg Pollard.'

'What does he do?'

'Something to do with travel, I think.'

'You think? You don't *know*?'

'Well, I haven't met him yet,' she said, nettled.

'What is this—a blind date set up by a friend? Or did you advertise in the personal column?'

'No, of course not.' She treated his sarcasm with the contempt it deserved. 'I've joined a computer dating service,' she said, proud of her bold initiative. 'They security-screen their clients and guarantee a seventy-five per cent compatibility rating—'

'*Computer dating!*'

'I thought you said he never shouted,' said Harriet to Nicola, who was looking at her father's red face in fascination.

He recovered his control with admirable swiftness, not even bothering to notice the ripples of interest that he had created at surrounding tables.

'I'm sorry but—dammit, Harriet,' he burst out softly, 'do you know what an incredible risk you're taking? A computer can't make character judgements; it's totally reliant on people being honest about themselves on the input data. No matter how well they're run, those kinds of organisations are rich feeding-grounds for con men and psychos who prey on the hopes and dreams of lonely, desperate people—'

'Greg sounded very nice on the phone—'

He dropped his knife. 'You gave him your *phone* number?'

'For goodness' sake, I'm not that stupid! The service gave me his number and *I* rang *him . . .*'

The rest of the lunch gave Harriet a very bad case of indigestion as she was forced to dine on Marcus's quiet, compelling lecture on the dangers of being too trusting.

By the time the embarrassingly large bill arrived twenty minutes later even Nicola was beginning to look a little shell-shocked, and it was small consolation when she confided later that afternoon that Harriet was the first person she had seen discompose her father so completely.

CHAPTER SEVEN

HARRIET sprawled backwards onto the luxuriously soft bed and stared up at the recessed lights in the cream-coloured ceiling with a smile of glorious anticipation.

She couldn't believe her luck to find such a marvellous apartment on the first day of looking and at such a good price was little short of a miracle. She must remember to buy Nicola a small gift of appreciation, for it was she who had mentioned that there were apartments in the Harbourside Building being advertised for sale and lease.

To Harriet, who had been at a loss as to where to begin the apartment-hunting expedition that she had boldly proposed for lunchtime on Monday, it had seemed like fate.

And so it had proved. She had been instantly enchanted by the dashing face-lift that the old building down near the city's waterfront had received, and the real-estate saleswoman who represented the vendor had been so friendly and enthusiastic and devoutly keen for Harriet to buy that she had impulsively agreed on the spot. All her instincts had told her that the light and airy one-bedroomed apartment was the perfect setting for her new lifestyle.

Besides, the price was practically a steal, and the vendor had even given the real-estate agency permission to take a deposit to the value of a short-term lease if the buyer wanted to take immediate possession. If the sale fell through for any reason after Harriet had moved in, she would still have the three-month period of the lease to look around for something else.

The fact that she'd been able to move in immediately had been the real clincher. Leaving the only home she'd ever known was an emotional wrench that Harriet had wanted over and done with as soon as possible, but even she hadn't thought that it could be achieved in only two days!

Harriet rolled onto her side and propped her head up on her hand as she surveyed the spacious, high-ceilinged bedroom. Although she had only been here a couple of hours she loved her new home already; it was modern, with a hint of the gothic character that featured so strongly on the façade of the building.

The cream walls and carpets contrasted with the muted pastels of the mostly built-in furniture, and the price had included a few of the showroom pieces which had been used as a sales tool, so that moving in had largely been a matter of transferring her personal belongings and the contents of her kitchen, enabling her to offer her old furniture to a second-hand dealer as a house-lot. Harriet had paid a removal company to do most of the moving while she was at work, and a few round trips in the Porsche had taken care of the rest.

Harriet bounced off the bed. She might as well go and get the last of her bits and pieces from the car, and then she would make her ceremonial first meal in the lavishly equipped kitchen.

Her Porsche was parked in her very own parking space in the basement, and Harriet gave it a loving pat as she lifted out the cardboard carton of old books, photographs and nick-nacks that had survived her ruthless house-clearing.

She was humming as she got back into the lift and bent to press the button for the right floor with her nose. She shifted her grip on the heavy carton as the lift paused at the ground floor, preparing a bright smile of greeting for one of her new neighbours, but when the doors opened her mouth rounded in a silent O as she saw the tall, familiar figure in a black suit instead of an intriguing stranger.

'Hello, Marcus!' she said breathlessly, recovering from her split second of disorientation.

'Good evening, Harriet,' he said gravely. She was suddenly glad that she had the box to hide behind, for Marcus's elegance reminded her that she had dressed comfortably for the move, in a thin white T-shirt, jeans and sandals and a headband made out of a scarf to keep her hair out of her eyes. Marcus had his briefcase with him, she noticed, so he was obviously on his way home from work.

Her heart began to pump madly again. 'Have you come to see me? I didn't think you knew—' She had presumed from his conspicuous lack of interference over the past couple of days that his daughter hadn't reported Harriet's latest extravagant impulse. She hadn't expected her to last out for so long.

'I suppose Nicola told you I was moving in this evening? Is she with you?' She peered around him, but there was no sign of anyone else in the tiled foyer except the young security guard, who was watching them curiously. 'I'm not really settled yet although I've moved almost everything in—I was just getting the last of my stuff from the car. You'll be my first visitor—'

'You shouldn't be carrying heavy weights like that.' Marcus cut through her nervous chatter and stepped into the lift, removing the carton from her slender arms.

'Really—it isn't very heavy,' Harriet protested, but she didn't bother to try to retrieve the box. By now she was used to the futility of arguing with Marcus's chivalrous instincts.

He had certainly got his way over the Porsche, turning up on her doorstep on Monday morning just as she was preparing to leave for work and politely commanding her to drive him to the office while his chauffeur, who had dropped him off, took the Volvo in for its service check.

Harriet had been tempted to give him the hair-raising ride of his life, but his tense air of resignation had led her to believe that that was just what he expected her to do, so she had perversely decided to give his conservative soul nothing to complain about. His detached comments had actually been quite helpful, although her thanks had been grudging because his smile and bland thanks for a smooth ride had made her realise that she had been neatly manipulated into behaving with depressing meekness.

'Heavy enough,' he said, tucking the carton easily under one arm. 'You should have asked someone to help instead of trying to carry it yourself.'

'I don't know anyone yet,' she said as the doors closed again.

'You know me,' he pointed out.

'I mean here, at the Harbourside,' she said, untying the bandanna and running a hand self-consciously through her untidy hair. 'I haven't seen any of my neighbours so far, but the saleswoman told me that most of the apartments are occupied.

'They're very sought-after, you know,' she boasted, her excitement about her new home brimming over now that she had someone to share it with. 'Mine is a corner one so I get two different views of the city; it's north-facing too, so I get the sun as well. As soon as I walked in I knew it was right for me so I bought it on the spot. And it's really a fabulous bargain. Even you couldn't have got a better deal!'

'I'm sure I couldn't,' he murmured equably, watching her deep-set eyes sparkle and her mouth curve widely with satisfaction.

When the lift halted at the fifth floor she led the way down the short hall, and he waited patiently while she dealt with the unfamiliar lock and threw open the door with a flourish.

'Well, what do you think?' she said eagerly, when he was hardly inside the door. 'Isn't it terrific?' She basked in self-satisfaction, not giving him a chance to reply. 'There's only one bedroom but the living areas are big and there's plenty of room for parties, and for guests to stay over—'

'Life is going to be one mad, social whirl for you, isn't it?' said Marcus, setting the carton carefully down on the honey-coloured dining table that had come with the apartment and placing his briefcase on the floor. As she moved restlessly under his steady blue gaze he asked smoothly, 'May I look around?'

The thought of showing him her bedroom gave her a strange curling sensation in her stomach. 'Yes, of course. Go ahead,' she said, waving vaguely in the direction of the rest of the apartment.

His dark head tilted to one side. 'Aren't you going to show me?'

It was as if he knew what she was feeling. 'I don't think you'll get lost,' she said tartly, taking refuge in a hostessy smile. 'I'll get us a drink while you're looking. What would you like?'

'A fruit juice, if you have it.'

'I have everything,' she said emphatically, thinking of the lavish array of bottles now residing in her drinks cabinet, awaiting the flood of new friends that she intended to make.

He looked around at the pale room, tinted a rich gold by the evening sun. 'It's a beautifully warm room...may I take off my jacket?'

For no reason at all his polite request made her blush. 'Of course... here, let me hang it up for you.' She took it from him and he turned away, loosening his collar and tie with a grunt of relief.

The ultra-fine wool fabric was still warm from his body and Harriet thrust it hurriedly into the closet by the door, deciding that she had better stick to orange juice too. Celebrating her unexpected first visitor with anything more potent would be asking for trouble. Marcus's mere presence made her feel light-headed enough—she didn't need the added stimulation of alcohol.

'How did your date go last night?'

The jacket almost slid off the hanger onto the floor. 'You mean with Greg Pollard? Fine. It went fine.'

'What was he like?' he said.

She continued to arrange the jacket to her satisfaction, keeping her back to him as she grimaced and made an effort to sound enthusiastic. 'Nice. He was very nice.'

'That sounds rather bland.'

Harriet shut the closet door rather more firmly than was necessary and turned around, hands on hips. 'Well, it wasn't. Greg and I had a very nice evening!'

She winced as she saw the corner of his mouth flicker. She had used that wretched word again. *Nice*. The trouble was that it described Greg perfectly. He had brimmed over with such niceness that she couldn't view him in a sexual context. As a candidate for a wild sexual fling, when it came to the crunch he had turned out to be even less appealing than Michael Fleet!

'Where did you go?'

'Just to dinner and a movie.'

'How nice.'

Harriet scowled at his innocent expression. 'It was even nicer when we went back to his flat and made mad, passionate love for the rest of the night!' she declared rashly.

He pursed his lips. 'No wonder you're looking a little washed out today.' It was evident that he didn't believe her, damn him! 'Perhaps you should save your stormy nights of unbridled lust for the weekends... if you can find time between hikes, that is. I understand that you corrupted several Scouts with an orgy of marshmallow-eating on your weekend away.'

She wished that she hadn't tried to give Nicola fits of appreciative giggles with stories of her trip—particularly the distressing fact that most of the hikers had been women.

'The Scout-leader was there too,' Harriet informed him sweetly, crossing her fingers in the folds of her T-shirt in the hope that Nicola hadn't gone into specifics. 'Hunky, hairy outdoor types really turn me on.'

He stretched his arms behind his head and rolled his shoulders slowly, easing out the tensions of the long day.

'If your taste runs to butch females no wonder poor Pollard bored you to tears last night.'

Harriet flushed at the lazy amusement in his voice. So Nicola had even mentioned that the scouts had been led by a woman. 'Don't you and your daughter have anything more interesting to do than discuss every minute detail of my activities?' she gritted.

He dropped his arms, smiling at her chagrin. 'Not at the moment, no. Nicola talks about you a lot. I think she's rather fascinated by your colourful activities and awed by your appetite for life... not to mention your glorious disrespect for my dignity,' he added wryly.

'My activities would be a lot more colourful if she wasn't shadowing me like a conscience every day,' Harriet said darkly. Actually it was fun to have someone to show off to—someone who hadn't known the old Harriet, who didn't poke and probe and ask awkward questions but accepted her as the person she was now.

'Your restraint is duly noted,' he said gravely. 'Nicola doesn't make friends easily but she seems to respond naturally to you, perhaps because you haven't tried to pressure her into liking you. She says you treat her as an equal and she likes that. Her grandmother has a tendency to be domineering, and her schoolteachers are the only other adult women with whom she's had close contact. As an only child she's been a bit lonely, I'm afraid.'

There was an odd note in his voice that made her ask, 'Haven't you ever been tempted to marry again?'

'For Nicola's sake? No,' he said discouragingly.

But he didn't tell her that it was none of her business so she murmured recklessly, 'Is that because you're still in love with your wife or because you enjoy your personal freedom too much?'

Instead of being embarrassed, as she had intended, he looked amused at the thrust. 'What ever makes you think I'm pining for Serena?'

She stepped behind one of the dining chairs, subconsciously putting a barrier between them.

'I don't know...perhaps the way that Nicola talks so freely about her. About how beautiful she was and how happy you were together...'

'Nicola doesn't even remember her mother. Most of her memories have been implanted by Susan, so naturally they're flattering ones, although I will admit that Serena was extremely beautiful.'

'She was blonde, wasn't she?'

'Courtesy of her hairdresser, yes. A genuine, platinum-plated bitch.' He smiled cynically at Harriet's heightened colour. 'That was what you wanted to know, wasn't it? And yes, I thought both of us were in love when I married her. I was too naïve at the time to realise that what Serena loved wasn't me specifically but male admiration in general, and that one man would never be able to provide enough to satisfy her craving. Her favourite game was to play her courtiers off against each other. Nothing pleased Serena more than being able to provoke an admirer into a fit of jealousy.'

Harriet tried, and failed, to imagine Marcus Fox in the grip of a jealous rage.

Her expression must have given her away because he said wryly, 'I was only twenty, and far too arrogant to accept my mistake gracefully. I persisted in believing we could make the marriage work. We had some monstrous rows before I realised that Serena was using my pride and my temper to keep me out of her bed so that she had some self-justification for her behaviour.

'She was never technically unfaithful but she had no intention of giving up her numerous men-friends, not even after Nicola was born—or should I say *especially* after Nicola was born? It's ironic that I should have married a woman so much like my mother...'

Harriet blinked at this insult. 'I thought your mother was a saint?' she blurted out, remembering what he had told her the other night.

'I'm talking about my natural mother. My father got a young woman pregnant just before he married Mum. By all accounts she was as irresponsible as they come— beautiful but dumb, except where men were concerned. When she fronted up to Mum after the wedding, asking for money, Mum persuaded her not to have an abortion. When I was born it was Mum who took me home from the hospital...my birth-mother just wanted to forget I existed.

'I can forgive her lack of intelligence and even her lack of maternal feelings, but I can't forgive her for flitting in and out of my childhood whenever she was

bored or broke, fawning over me and claiming she'd
never wanted to give me up, refusing to allow Mum the
status of being my legal mother. I was only about six
when they told me she'd been killed in an accident but
I remember feeling glad that she was never coming back.'

'I don't suppose *she* was a bleached blonde too, by
any chance?' said Harriet flippantly, to hide how appalled she was by his matter-of-fact account of what must
have been an emotional turmoil. Having grown up in a
deeply loving, traditional family, she couldn't com-
prehend the idea of not wanting your own child.

She felt mortified when he confirmed cynically, 'How
perceptive of you to guess, Dr Smith. I have photographs from her abortive modelling career that show her
as the archetypal bimbo—all pouting lips and breasts
and a mass of teased hair. And that was in the days
when bleaching your hair instantly identified a woman
as either a cheap floozy or an expensive tart.'

Harriet's hand rose automatically to her hair. 'So that's
why you have a thing about blondes,' she murmured,
tucking a curl nervously behind her ear, her heart aching
for the boy who had despised the woman who had borne
him. 'Because of your unresolved feelings about your
mother—'

'Don't tell me you're taking night classes in psycho-
analysis too,' he said with a distinct edge. 'I suppose
you're going to try and hang an Oedipus complex on
me next, or tell me I was trying to return to the security
of the womb when I married Serena.'

Since that was precisely the kind of psychobabble that
had been passing through her mind, Harriet flushed. 'If
you're still that touchy about it, maybe you *should* consider therapy,' she said, reminding herself that he was
now a fully grown man in total control of his life, and
in no need of her misplaced sympathy.

'Why? A human being's most valuable asset is the ability to learn from experience and thus not be condemned to endlessly repeating his mistakes.'

'Two blondes amongst millions of women who artificially lighten their hair don't actually amount to much experience,' she pointed out scathingly.

'Oh, there were a few others along the way who contributed to my disillusionment... women who thought my fatal weakness for their synthetic golden looks would forgive them anything. I've since realised that a truly sensual woman doesn't have to flaunt her sexuality; her appeal is much more subtle... and enduring. Unfortunately such women appear to be a rarity in these strident times...'

Was that a dig at her? How many treacherous blondes had it taken to disillusion him, for goodness' sake? For an intelligent man he must be a slow learner. Harriet felt an ugly emotion boiling up inside her that she knew, with a touch of panic, was jealousy. Fortunately, before it could spill over and scald them both, Marcus said smoothly, 'So... have you made arrangements to see the boring Mr Pollard again?'

The sudden switch back to his original subject caught Harriet completely off guard and she hesitated a moment too long.

Marcus's face was harsh with satisfaction as he nodded. 'I guess not. What's wrong, Harriet? Didn't he conform to your computerised specifications? What exactly did you ask for on that ridiculous form you filled in?'

'A stud!' she told him, still angry with him for making her feel things that he had no right to make her feel.

'You want to get pregnant?' he murmured, eyes dropping to her flat belly.

She gasped, taking a step backwards. 'No, of course not! I mean a stud in the slang sense!'

'Slang sense?'

Her chest heaved with outrage under the white T-shirt but she answered him anyway, since it was just possible that a stuffy conservative really wouldn't know the modern slang. 'As in a man who's young, handsome and virile and exciting!' Seeing his jaw jut dangerously, she warmed to her theme. 'Someone who doesn't have any emotional attachments and won't make a nuisance of himself afterwards.'

'Afterwards?'

She managed not to blush. 'The next morning!' she flung at him defiantly.

His gaze wandered slowly up from her waist, his thick, dark lashes screening his expression. 'So what's next on the agenda? Or should I say who? Has the computer lined you up with another white-hot prospect for tonight?'

She was frustrated by his lack of reaction. 'Tomorrow night, actually. Tonight I have a class.'

'I thought that was Monday.'

'Monday is French. Wednesday is car maintenance.'

He looked alarmed. 'You're not going to try to service the Porsche yourself?'

She almost laughed at his expression. 'Your chauvinism is showing; but no, this is just a hobby... a way to meet people.'

'You mean men,' he said bluntly, his eyes narrowing. 'All these classes you're taking aren't just about expanding your interests, are they, Harriet? They're a way for you to meet a few more wham-bam-thank-you-Sams!'

'I see your grasp of slang has improved radically in the last few minutes,' she snapped. 'So what if they are? What makes you the guardian of my morality?'

'Don't tempt me,' he growled bafflingly.

'I wouldn't bother to try. You're not my type!'

'I don't think you know what your type is, Harriet; that's the problem...'

'*You* may see it as a problem—*I* see it as a challenge,' she said with a reckless toss of her head. 'After all, looking is half the fun of the game—'

'But you're not really looking for fun, you're looking for forgetfulness,' he said with a quiet certainty that struck her to the heart. 'And I'm afraid you won't find it in meaningless sexual encounters. If anything you'll discover an even more corrosive form of loneliness—'

'I thought you said you wanted to look around the apartment,' she interrupted fiercely, not wanting to hear any more. 'I'm going to get the drinks.'

She half expected him to trail her into the kitchen to continue cutting at her fragile composure, but to her unutterable relief she heard the quiet rustle of his footsteps as he prowled briefly around the lounge and then deeper into the back of the apartment.

By the time she carried the tray of drinks and dishes of olives and cheese out into the living room she felt ready to face him again, but to her surprise Marcus still hadn't reappeared from his self-guided tour.

What was he doing? she wondered as she anxiously sipped her drink. What had he found to interest him for so long? When she could bear the tension no longer she walked cautiously towards the bedroom, ready to beat a hasty retreat if she heard him in the bathroom.

She found him sitting on the edge of her bed, engrossed in a book from the stack on top of her bedside cabinet—the result of her whirlwind unpacking.

He looked up as she hovered warily in the doorway.

'*How To Turn Your Life Around*?' His mouth curved wryly. 'I thought you had already worked that out to your satisfaction.' He turned his attention to the rest of the books, which still bore their price stickers, and began to sort through them. 'Mmm, your bedtime reading is

very instructive—*How To Be The Woman You Are,
Blondes Have More Fun*—two contradictory titles there!
And what's this? *How To Attract Men.* I would have
thought that was rather superfluous for you too, since
you became a sizzling platinum blonde...'

Sizzling? Intent on preventing him from reaching the
bottom of the pile, Harriet hastened forward, but she
was too late. His eyebrows shot up as he studied the
final cover.

'*Sexual Fulfilment: Erotic Techniques To Enhance
Female Pleasure.*'

'Give me that!' Flustered, she tried to snatch it out
of his hand.

'Give you what? Sexual fulfilment?' he enquired with
a wicked grin, easily evading her attack by catching her
wrist and pulling her down onto the bed beside him.
'Why, Harriet, I'm flattered by your eagerness but it's
rude to grab.'

'I meant give me the book!' she grated at him, feeling
the heat of his thigh against her hip as they bounced
lightly together on the edge of the bed.

'Why? Do you think I'd be shocked?'

To her dismay he flicked the book on his lap open at
random, and they both looked down at the explicit colour
drawing which accompanied the test.

'Goodness!' he murmured, with fine restraint. The
woman was blonde, the man dark-haired and lithely
muscular. Harriet wondered hectically if he had blue
eyes. She tore her gaze from the erotic blending of male
and female on the page and looked helplessly at Marcus.
His eyelids had drooped and a slightly dreamy look of
fascination softened his hard face. A faint tinge of
redness stole into his cheeks as the seconds ticked by,
and a pulse began to throb heavily at his temple.

He slowly turned the page. The whisper of paper sounded loud in the quiet room. He turned another and she saw his nostrils flare as he inhaled sharply.

'Goodness,' he murmured again, and lifted his head. Their eyes clashed and his were darkly brilliant, but not, she knew, with shock.

'You aren't looking,' he accused thickly.

'Yes, I am.' The dazed words were out before she could stop them. 'I mean—'

His eyes flared with triumph.

'I know exactly what you mean,' he growled, spilling the book off his lap onto the floor as he half turned to reach for her, dragging her against his chest.

'You're looking with your mind,' he said huskily against her mouth, 'and your mind can see you and me doing to each other what that man and woman are doing...only we're not frozen into position on the pages of a book. We can move. We're real, warm and alive and so is this...'

He kissed her deep and hard, burying his mouth in hers, using his teeth to tease her lips apart and his tongue to thrust roughly inside. His hand slid from her upper arms to her ribcage, his fingers splaying up her slender sides, gripping her, supporting her torso while he slowly twisted from side to side, massaging her breasts with the rigid muscles of his chest. With a groan he turned her even further into the heated embrace, forcing her head back with the power of his kiss, lifting his knee to rest his thigh heavily across her sprawled legs, urging her against the hardness between his legs.

'Kiss me; touch me the way she was touching him.' He whispered the ragged command into the moist depths of her being, and she felt him tear at his buttons so that his shirt parted across his smooth, hot chest. Then his fingers were sliding against her T-shirt, pulling it free from the top of her jeans, the pads of his fingertips rasping like rough satin against her bare skin.

'Marcus—'

He bit her throat, his fingers curving into her soft waist as he sucked at her flesh. 'Yes, say my name; tell me where you want me to stroke you; tell me what excites you...'

Everything excited her. She could barely string two coherent thoughts together, let alone utter any words. All that came from her lungs were gasps and tiny whimpers and moans that seemed to drive him into a greater frenzy.

Harriet clutched at the thick-hewn shoulders under the loose white shirt, her manicured nails biting into the rippling muscle and raking down his biceps, causing him to arch and shudder and rub himself more frantically against her. The heat was coming off him in waves, the muscles in his arms and chest jerking with convulsive tension, his hot mouth ravishing her senses as he hungrily devoured her response to his astonishing explosion of desire.

Almost as exciting as his touch was the knowledge that he was no longer in control of himself. The polite, courteous protector had disappeared, leaving a man in the grip of a primitive, driving passion. He was shaking with it... sweating with it, his skin growing slippery beneath Harriet's hands.

She licked the salt from his collar-bone and he uttered a harsh cry and toppled like a mighty oak, taking her down sideways onto the bed as his hands found her rounded breasts beneath the T-shirt.

'I knew you weren't wearing a bra,' he muttered harshly, covering the delicate mounds with his palms, cupping and shaping her with his fingers, finding the soft nipples with his thumbs and tracing their outline by feel, circling them over and over again, drawing them out with the gentle pressure of his nails. 'I could see these shadowed against the cotton...dark, smooth, round discs that I wanted to touch and lick and suck until they were ripe and wet and hard...as hard as I was...'

He nuzzled her mouth as he told her what else he had wanted to do to her breasts with his tongue and hands and body while she had been standing there talking, innocently unaware of his lustful fancies, and his eloquent description made Harriet so dizzy that if she hadn't been lying down she would have swooned like a Victorian maiden.

She couldn't believe that it was cool, contained Marcus Fox saying these things to her—raw, explicit, sexual things that should have made her melt with embarrassment but which sent hot bolts of pleasure shafting through her breasts and belly until her whole body throbbed with feverish anticipation.

She was almost sobbing with frustration by the time he pushed the T-shirt up over her breasts, thrusting her onto her back with the weight of his body, one thigh wedging heavily between hers as he braced himself on his elbow half over her.

'Yes...oh, God, yes,' he said hoarsely as he framed one breast in his fingers, preparing to shape her for his mouth. 'Such lovely, big nipples for such small, delicate breasts..,they quite enchant me...' His fingers contracted firmly and he bent to dampen the jutting tip with his tongue. 'Ah, yes, and they're so very, very sensitive, aren't they, darling? Exquisitely, beautifully sensitive. I know they are, and I promise I'll be very, very careful not to let you come before you're ready this time...'

Time was meaningless to Harriet. She heard his words through a thin veil of red mist, giving a ragged cry and arching her spine as she felt his mouth moistly envelop her in unspeakable pleasure. He moved from one breast to the other and it was just like her dream . . . better than her imagination . . . Marcus over her, his rumpled shirt hanging open, his chest rippling with each savage undulation of his hips as he moved on her, pushing down between her thighs with slow, grinding thrusts, building a familiar violent tension that made her thresh and moan. It had never been like this before, *never*. Keith had never roused her to such heights, and so how could it be familiar? And yet . . . and yet . . .

She cried out Marcus's name, her intense yearning mingled with bewilderment.

He stiffened, and responded by seeming to drag himself back from the brink of that unnamed violence.

'I know, I know . . . you wonder what's happening to us,' he soothed raggedly, returning to nip and suck at her swollen mouth, fondling her with his darting tongue. 'It feels so incredibly right, doesn't it, to be with me like this . . . as if we know exactly how to please each other without having to be told, without needing a book of instructions . . . ?'

His hand moved down to plunge between her thighs, his finger testing the inner seam of her jeans, rubbing the ridge of denim lightly against her most sensitive woman's flesh. She gasped, and he dipped and drank the sound from her lips.

His finger moved again, scraping back and forth, and his mouth hovered invitingly. 'Yes . . . it's strong, isn't it? If you want to live by your instincts, Harriet, ask yourself what your instincts are telling you now . . . Why don't you show me just how daring my reckless blonde can be?'

CHAPTER EIGHT

'*No!*'

Harriet took them both by surprise by shoving at him with a burst of superhuman strength. He reared back and she half scrambled, half fell off the side of bed, landing with a jolting thud on her bottom. She lay there, panting, staring up at him in a state of deep shock.

A 'reckless blonde'. Knowing what she was should have made his blood run cold, not hot. His cynical mistrust was her best protection against her own wayward desires.

Marcus sat staring back. His face was dark with blood, his powerful body bunched and aggressive, his cool eyes a molten blue. His close-cut black hair stood up in little spikes and his glistening chest was heaving. He looked like a wild man.

He bent, extending his hand towards her, and Harriet scooted back on her bottom.

'No, don't touch me!'

There was a stinging pause. 'It's a little late for that, isn't it, Harriet?'

He was looking at her bare breasts and she felt a fresh rush of heat as she dragged down the T-shirt that was rucked up under her arms, trying not to notice how it caught and clung to the dampened peaks.

'It's never too late to say no,' she said raggedly.

'At the risk of being accused of not being a gentleman—that's not true,' he said with dangerous softness. 'There's a definite point of no return for both men and women...and we weren't very far from reaching

139

it.' His hand remained extended. 'Here, let me help you up.'

She didn't trust herself to touch him. She got to her knees, and then wavered to her feet. He got off the bed, moving slowly, making no attempt to button his shirt. The smooth olive of his chest was marred in several places by red smudges, and Harriet was horrified to realise that they were the marks left by her teeth when she had bitten him in the throes of her violent excitement. There were claw marks too, across one shoulder and down his arm. She remembered his thick groan when she had done it and wondered sickly if she had hurt him...

Frightened by the pain that the thought caused, she said baldly, 'I think you should go now...'

She turned and walked unsteadily back to the lounge, where she dragged his jacket out of the closet and held it out to him.

'Why? Have I offended you?' he murmured, crooking his arm to catch the jacket as she let it fall. She couldn't stop looking at his chest and he glanced down and ruefully touched one of the red marks, just below his glossy brown nipple.

'Were we too rough? I should have warned you that I tend towards a certain primitiveness in my lovemaking, perhaps because the rest of my life is necessarily so highly civilised.' His fingers drifted lightly across his skin. 'Somehow you make me feel even more vulnerable, stripped of every ounce of control and inhibition.'

Harriet stiffened, fighting off an attack of dizzying panic. She didn't want to be responsible for anyone's feelings, not when she couldn't even cope with her own...

'That's because you don't really trust me. You can't; how can you? I'm a *blonde*! She said it in the same awful tones she might have used to announce that she was a bride of Satan.

'I *had* noticed,' he said drily.

'Of course you had.' She clutched at the straw. 'Maybe that's the problem...maybe it was my hair that triggered you off. We were talking about your disillusionment with synthetic blondes, and you were remembering...and then you were looking at—at those pictures in the book and...and, well, maybe you're not quite as cured of your—uh—fatal weakness as you thought you were,' she ended lamely.

It sounded thin even to her own ears and she watched nervously as he quietly began to button up his shirt with his free hand.

He didn't hurry, and he finished by neatly tucking the tails under his narrow belt before commenting finally, 'Interesting theory. Of course, that doesn't explain *your* behaviour. You melted like wax the moment I touched you...you were mine every step of the way—until you got a bad case of cold feet.'

'That's not what happened—'

'I was there; I know what happened; and I know why,' he added, picking up his briefcase and strolling over to the door. 'Face it, Harriet, you're not and never will be a genuine risk-taker. You don't have the temperament for living life on the edge. You'll always think of a logical reason to hold yourself back, to do the sensible thing. You're so busy running that you haven't even bothered to look around and see that what you're so frightened of is only a chimera—'

'I'm not running from anything,' she cried angrily, marching after him.

He paused, hand on the doorknob. 'No? Let's put that to the test, shall we? I dare you to cancel your date with Sam tomorrow night and have dinner with me.'

'It's Nigel,' she retorted hotly. 'And if you think you can manipulate me with a childish ploy like that you're very much mistaken.'

* * *

So how was it that the next night, instead of painting the town red with Nigel, she was dining by candlelight at the Fox residence, eating glazed lamb cutlets and sedately carrying on a conversation with a complacent and relaxed Marcus and his well-mannered daughter?

Harriet wasn't quite certain herself; she only knew that Marcus was far more skilled than she at winning arguments and an expert at burying his opponent in confusion.

Tonight, for instance, when she had driven up to his imposing residence, primed for battle and dressed accordingly in a severe black dress that covered her from throat to ankle, emphasising the uncompromising whiteness of her hair, she had been taken aback to be welcomed by Nicola, serenely playing hostess for her father.

It had been Nicola who had shown her around the beautiful old house, with its ornate, high ceilings and gracious rooms filled with lovingly cared-for antiques, Nicola who had brought her a pre-dinner drink and generated the small talk that bridged the initial awkward gap between Harriet and her unexpectedly reticent host.

Harriet's intention to behave badly and make Marcus regret ever having forced the invitation had died without a whimper when she'd found out that Nicola had not only been responsible for the romantic table setting in the sumptuous dining room, but had also helped prepare the meal and took her social duties very seriously.

'Granny says that every woman should know the key elements of giving a good dinner party,' she'd said as she'd shown them their places at the table with a mixture of naïve pride and maturity. And Daddy said it's a useful business tool to have the ability to put people at ease in a social setting.'

'Even for a filing clerk,' Marcus had teased gently, waiting until the two ladies were seated before sitting down himself.

'I won't always be a filing clerk,' Nicola had pointed out, and the conversation had flowed into a discussion of what else she might be, given the options available to her, and Harriet had been startled to find her own opinions solicited and dwelt on as if she actually had influence on the matter.

Against all odds, Harriet found herself relaxing and forgetting that she was supposed to be here under duress. It was a bitter-sweet experience to find herself dining once more *en famille*, talking about events both momentous and mundane. Meals after her mother's death had tended to be scrappy, due to her father's lack of interest in anything other than his grief, and later he had been too ill to sit at the table.

'Glad you decided to change your mind after all?' Marcus leaned towards her at one point to murmur, the stern lines of his face flattered by the candlelight, the smile on his lips echoed in his eyes.

She didn't have to ask what he meant. 'Oh, is that what happened?' Harriet replied with gentle sarcasm, conscious of a faint anxiety in Nicola's observant gaze, as if she sensed the surging undercurrents.

'Well, you're here now, and that's all that matters...' Was it? Why?

She couldn't make him out. He had been charming, urbane and kind. He had said nothing that was designed to make her feel nervous or uncomfortable... and still he seemed to grow ever more threatening in her awareness. He had dressed formally, and so had Nicola, and yet his manner was flatteringly informal...the three of them, laughing and talking around the table, being served by a smiling housekeeper to whom Harriet was introduced on a first-name basis.

When father and daughter excluded her with jokes and references to people that Harriet didn't know, Marcus would pause and give her amusing thumbnail descriptions of their characters, drawing her back into the conversation.

When the talk drifted to the merits of being only children it seemed natural to tell them about her elder brother—how she had shared her parents' terror of Tim's daredevil exploits, and had felt overshadowed by the sheer exuberance of his personality. He had graduated over the years from climbing the highest tree and diving from the highest board to skydiving, climbing mountains, bungee jumping from helicopters and, just before he'd died, had taken up extreme skiing.

'You mean I won't get to meet him?' said Nicola, with typically youthful self-absorption. 'How long ago did he die?'

'Two years ago.' Harriet didn't look at Marcus, but out of the corner of her eye she saw his hand still on his water glass, his knuckles whitening under invisible pressure.

'What happened? Was he killed on a mountain or something?' Nicola asked.

'No, that was what was so ironic. He came down with what he thought was a mild flu and twenty-four hours later he was dead,' she said quietly. 'It happened so fast . . . some virulent form of meningitis. All those years of Mum and Dad living in fear of a late-night phone call from some God-forsaken spot on the other side of the world, and he dies at home from an infection that could have been cured if he hadn't been so stoical and refused to go to the doctor. By the time we took him to the hospital it was too late. I don't think Mum ever forgave herself. I think that's what brought on her stroke.'

She blinked rapidly and took a hasty sip of her sparkling mineral water, but instead of politely pretending to ignore her embarrassing lapse, as most people were inclined to do when unexpectedly confronted with the subject of death, Marcus encouraged her to continue. He pointedly asked her if Tim had also outshone her at school, and Harriet had to smile at his chagrin when she answered wryly, 'As a matter of fact, yes. He was a brilliant all-rounder, while I'm afraid I was ordinary at everything. A little brown sparrow to his peacock... that's what my mother used to call us.'

He had obviously expected her answer to be in the negative. He had been trying to apply balm to her wounded childhood ego. Harriet was secretly touched, although she maintained her outward amusement.

As the leisurely evening drew on she realised in despair that liking Marcus Fox was the least of her problems. She was very much afraid that the emotions already ran far deeper than that. If so, her freedom was going to prove just as much an illusion as her former security had been.

They didn't have dessert until after the housekeeper had retired, and Harriet went with Nicola to fetch it from the kitchen.

'Are you going to stay the night?' Nicola asked, putting the tray of raspberry tartlets into the oven to warm briefly.

Harriet almost dropped the crystal dish of cream that she had been asked to get from the fridge.

'No, of course not!' She couldn't stop the urgent question spilling out. 'Does your father often have dinner guests stay over?'

Nicola smiled. An unnervingly adult smile. 'If you mean women, no.'

Harriet stiffened. 'Not that it matters to me.'

Nicola leaned against the bench. Her hair had been wound on top of her head and her rust-coloured dress was one that Harriet had helped her buy—youthful, yet more sophisticated than her usual jejune style. Her expression behind her glasses was alarmingly frank. 'It matters to Granny. She's always asking me about Daddy's girlfriends.'

'I'm sorry. I didn't meant to pry,' Harriet replied. God forbid that she should be anything like that blue-rinsed drill-sergeant!

'Actually, Daddy's never had a woman to stay while I've been here. He's awfully discreet. I think he's afraid that I'll be corrupted for ever if I find out my father has an active sex life.'

'Nicola!'

'Well, I'm fifteen—I do know about these things even if Daddy likes to pretend I don't.'

The timer pinged and she turned her back on Harriet's gaping face to pick up the oven glove.

'But Mummy's been dead for ten years and I don't expect he's been celibate all that time, do you?' she said, removing the tarts from the oven. 'I mean, it wouldn't be natural, would it? I don't suppose that you inviting him round to your place last night means you and Daddy are . . . ?' She trailed off with heavy-handed delicacy, her eyes rising suggestively over the tops of her spectacle rims.

Harriet went red. '*No!* And I didn't invite him. He simply turned up.'

'I just wondered.' She arranged the hot tartlets on the dessert plates with deft fingers. 'You don't have to worry about me, you know . . . if you were thinking about it. I wouldn't mind.'

Harriet was going hot and cold with embarrassment. If she was that transparent to a *child*, how much did everyone else see? Maybe that explained the people who had been just 'popping in' to the file room in the last couple of days. She shoved the ghastly thought away.

'Really, Nicola, you have a very weird imagination. Your father and I are totally incompatible!'

Nicola looked at her pityingly. 'Sex isn't about compatibility—even *I* know that. It's about animal magnetism and the survival of the species!'

Harriet was still brooding over that highly simplistic interpretation an hour later as she sat in the passenger seat of her Porsche and watched Marcus having a few last words with his daughter on the doorstep of the elegantly sprawling house. Bringing her own car had not prevented Marcus from playing the gentleman to the hilt and insisting on driving her home, pointing out that the generous amount of liqueur she had enjoyed in her coffee might have her teetering on the edge of the legal limit. They were also twenty minutes out in the country, along winding, narrow, unlit roads that were unfamiliar to her in daylight, let alone on a cloudy night with no moon.

Harriet doubted that her faculties were in the slightest impaired, but she knew that she couldn't be seen to take the slightest risk with Nicola looking on. The message that alcohol and driving didn't mix had to be applied to everyone to be effective.

'Or you could stay the night,' Marcus had said blandly, and as she'd hurriedly refused Nicola had uttered a snicker that had made Harriet want to throttle her.

'What were you saying to her?' Harriet said sharply as Marcus swung himself behind the wheel and waved to his daughter as she closed the front door. Whatever it was, it had taken a long time.

'That rather than get a taxi back I'll probably stay in town.'

Harriet groaned inwardly. She could just imagine what Nicola was thinking now! 'He's awfully discreet...'

'Not with me you won't!'

'Why, Harriet, did I suggest that?' he murmured innocently. 'I have my own apartment. I told Nicola I'll phone her as soon as I get there.'

She had never seen his personal quarters in the Finance Tower, but Nicola had told her that he stayed there quite often when she was away at school, sometimes only making it home at weekends.

He turned the key and gave a sigh as the engine throbbed into life. He turned on the headlights, and paused to give her a boyish smile that completely banished the threat of a frown that perpetually hovered in the forbidding black brows. 'You know, I really only asked you to dinner to get my hands on your Porsche. I knew you wouldn't let me drive it if I merely asked nicely.'

'I don't let anyone drive my car,' she said haughtily.

His smile turned into a grin. 'But I'm not just anyone, am I, blondie?'

He drove it superbly, as she'd known he would, and when he parked it in the Harbourside basement and pocketed the keys to follow her into the lift, she didn't say a word. He, too, seemed to feel no need to ask or explain. They both knew what was going to happen.

The silence was charged with tension as they stood side by side, watching the floor numbers changing on the digital counter. The sleeve of his jacket brushed the skin of her forearms and Harriet swayed, feeling as if she had been stroked by rivulets of fire. She could feel him looking at her and knew what he must be seeing— the flushed cheeks, the parted lips, the shallow rise and fall of her breasts—all the signs of a woman on the brink of surrender. By the time they reached her apartment door Harriet's palms were clammy, and she was aware of every inch of her body beneath the plain black jersey silk.

There was a dream-like sense of inevitability about what they were doing. Harriet suddenly knew that everything that had passed between them tonight...yesterday...the past week—everything from the moment he had barged into Brian Jessop's office nearly two weeks ago, and perhaps even before then...perhaps all of her *life*...had been leading to this one, glorious moment...

She opened her door and turned to him, breathlessly...

Marcus cupped her cheek and tilted her face towards his. He kissed her once on the brow and once on the mouth, very gently, and pressed her car keys into her hand.

'Goodnight, Harriet. Thank you for tonight. Sleep well.'

Sleep well?

Harriet stood in her doorway and watched him walk back to the lift.

Sleep well?

The doors were still open and he stepped in and pressed the button without looking back.

That was *it*?

He had brought her to this fever pitch of expectation and wanted her to go to *sleep*? 'Thank you for tonight'? What was there to thank her for? She hadn't done anything yet!

At first she thought that it must be a joke. That at the last minute before the doors closed he was going to turn and laugh, and come back and sweep her off her feet. Only when the lift had departed did she stumble into her apartment and shut the door and slam her back against the hard panels, trying to force the knowledge through her bones.

He had left her. He hadn't brought her home to make love to her. He had set out to control her, seduce her, beguile her, and now he didn't want her. She didn't want tenderness, damn him; she wanted what he had promised her yesterday... complete and utter oblivion.

Hot tears of humiliation burned at the back of her eyes and thickened her throat. Had he detected the sheer desperation of her need? Was that what had frightened him off? It frightened her—the realisation that to feel like making love she first had to make herself *feel* love. If sex and love were truly indivisible in her mind then that meant the only person she *could* have her wild, reckless fling with was Marcus. And if he didn't want her, where did that leave her wonderful new life?

Harriet put the back of her hand over her quivering mouth and bit it, hard, using the pain to fight back the creeping tendrils of depression. You couldn't lose something you never had, she repeated to herself. Look on the bright side, Harriet. What if the bastard had made love to you and *then* walked out?

She couldn't possibly be feeling this desperate over a man who had scarcely impinged on her consciousness a couple of weeks ago. It wasn't love, it was infatuation. She had been flattered by his attention, blown it up into something it wasn't.

She looked across at the glass door that led out onto her little balcony, at the shadowy blocks and bright lights of the city. *Her* city. If only she'd had a few hefty pot plants out there, she thought, feeding her healthy anger, she would very much have liked to drop one over the rail on the man who was probably stepping out into the street below right now to hail a taxi—

Harriet jerked upright. She whirled around and wrenched open the door, dashing out into the hall, to stare up at the indicator above the lift. It wasn't registering the lift on the ground floor. Instead, it showed it four floors above. She replayed the ghastly scene of Marcus's leaving in her mind. She hadn't noticed it then, but she remembered now. His hand had tapped the panel at chest-level. He had taken the lift up, not down.

What business could Marcus possibly have on the top floor at this time of night? Monkey business, she thought furiously, storming back into her apartment and snatching up the telephone to call the security office in the foyer, on the off chance that she might be wrong.

Fortunately the security guard who answered turned out to be the same one who had been on duty when she'd moved in.

'Oh, yes, Miss Smith.' His voice had the lilt of recognition when she identified her apartment number. 'I hope there's nothing wrong?'

'No...it's just that I wondered if you had seen Mr Fox go out...the man who was with me yesterday? He escorted me up from the car park a few minutes ago and was supposed to leave the building again straight away, but he's left something important in my apartment...' Namely Harriet!

'No, but then he might not have come through the foyer if he had his car in the basement. Shall I call Basement Security and see if they can stop him?'

'He hasn't got his car with him. I presumed he was going to get a taxi—'

'Oh. Then would you like me to try his penthouse for you? He usually calls a taxi from there and then rings down for us to notify him when it arrives...'

Five minutes later Harriet had her finger firmly on the bell of 901, trying to ignore the quaking in her stomach.

When Marcus opened the door she pushed roughly past him.

'*How dare you interfere in my life?*'

He sighed, tightening the belt on his long dark blue towelling robe. 'I take it you've just discovered that I live here too—'

'*Live* here? Security told me *you own the building*!' She raged further into his sprawling lair—much more luxurious than her own. He followed, his bare feet slapping lightly against the classic black and white tiles of the entranceway.

'A terrible crime, to be true. Couldn't this wait until morning, Harriet?'

The hint of impatience was fuel to the flame burning hot in her chest. 'No, it can't!' she said savagely. 'And don't bother to tell me you're too tired to listen, because Nicola told me that you never need much sleep.'

She came to a stop in the centre of a cool blue split-level lounge and, sure enough, there were papers spread out on the glass coffee-table, and a fountain pen casually uncapped beside them, as if it had just been thrown down.

Marcus had told her to 'sleep well' so that he could rush back to attend his long-established, much more fascinating mistress... his *work*!

She swung around, vibrating with outrage.

'I was thinking more for your sake than for mine,' he murmured. 'Wouldn't you like to mull this over before you say something we both might regret?'

'You set me up, didn't you?' she exploded furiously. 'No *wonder* that saleswoman fell over herself to sell me the apartment. She had orders from *you* to make sure I got it. No *wonder* it was such a good deal! And the irony is, I thought that I was exercising total freedom. I enjoyed knowing that I was buying a home by myself, *for* myself, for the first time in my life. But I wasn't even allowed to do that, was I? All along I was being manipulated by *you*...'

'It turned out for the best, though, didn't it?' he pointed out reasonably. 'You told me last night you love the apartment.'

Harriet clenched her fists at her sides to stop herself from hitting him.

'Best for whom? Did you feel *sorry* for me—was that it?' She hated the idea of being an object of his pity. 'Didn't you think I was *competent* enough to find my own place? Or was it just because you needed to have me firmly under her your thumb to be sure I wouldn't corrupt your precious daughter?' She laughed wildly. 'Yes, that's it, isn't it? You have to be in control of every*thing* and every*one* around you and you couldn't stand it when I wouldn't let you stifle me with your stuffy rules and expectations. You even stooped to using your daughter; you *told* her to bring me here, didn't you?'

'I *suggested* that she let you know there were apartments here for sale,' he corrected her evenly. 'The rest was largely the result of your own enthusiasm. The ultimate decision was yours. There was no cheating or coercion involved, certainly not on Nicola's part. I doubt that she knows I own the building. Nicola isn't privy to all my business dealings.'

'But she must know you have an apartment here. She could have told me that.'

'I told her that it might unfairly prejudice your decision if you knew, and I was correct, wasn't I?' he said harshly. 'It shouldn't have been relevant, but you would have denied yourself an apartment that was everything you wanted just because you're afraid to face what I represent. Your conscience eats at you when I'm around, doesn't it, Harriet? You want to be totally reckless but you can't quite escape the guilt. You thought you had all your reasons mapped out but now you're not sure. Poor Harriet, you're scared that I might curb your headlong rush into the arms of disaster—'

'You mean the arms of other men! That's what really bugs you, isn't it? It's not enough that you control where

I work and where I live,' she accused fiercely. 'Now you want to control my sex life too.'

He crossed his arms, the lapels of his robe splitting to reveal a narrow V of skin above the loose tie.

'If you mean your intention to engage in serial sex with a string of men whose only recommendation is what's between their legs,' he said through his teeth, 'then yes—I'll do everything in my power to stop you destroying what's left of your self-respect!'

Harriet went scarlet from head to toe with a searing shame that drove her to greater recklessness. 'You have no right to tell me who I can and cannot have sex with!' she shouted. 'I'll sleep my way through the telephone directory if I feel like it.'

'I certainly have more right than anyone else in your life, you stupid little bitch!' he shouted back, the veins in his temples throbbing dark red, the cords in his neck standing out.

'The hell you do! You can stuff your job. I quit!' she screamed. She turned and would have run for the door, except he caught her by the elbow in a punishing grip and wrenched her back around.

'Oh, no, you can't run away from this one. This is nothing to do with position or power. I don't *have* to control your sex life, Harriet, and do you know why?' He gave her a little shake. 'Because I *am* your sex life. The only lover you've had since that cretinous fiancé dumped you is *me*! On New Year's Eve!'

There was a strange buzzing in her ears and Harriet's mouth went completely dry. 'What do you mean?' she whispered. 'My God, what are you saying?'

He tempered his anger, his grip changing to one more supportive than imprisoning, but his voice was still implacably grim. 'I mean, my dear, that, while you don't seem to remember anything much about the staff party on New Year's Eve, my memory of what happened between us is somewhat more lucid.'

'I don't know what you're talking about...' Harriet said faintly, the blood draining out of her face.

He caught her other arm as she swayed, gently turning her in the direction of a long, low-backed leather couch. 'I know; that's the one redeeming feature of this whole ridiculous mess. At least you haven't been *consciously* trying to drive me insane. Come and sit down...'

She stiffened in resistance, clutching at his arm. 'No, tell me now,' she ordered wildly. 'I need to know *now*...'

'You need to sit down before you fall down.' He let go of her experimentally and her knees sagged. 'See?' he said, straightening her up again and urging her across the thick carpet. 'I'm not going to say anything else until you're safely sitting down.'

'You always have to control things...' she complained vaguely, concentrating her woolly mind on placing one foot in front of the other. Finally she could sink into the fat leather cushions and the horrid floating sensation turned into one of leaden dread.

He sat down beside her, chafing her icy hands.

'Only because I know there are so many *other* things that are completely out of my control. Like you totally blotting out what happened on New Year's Eve. You were very resistant whenever I tried to bring the subject up, but perhaps you'll tell me now—what *do* you remember about that party?'

She couldn't look at him. She looked down at her feet instead—plain black shoes set primly together. 'Nothing. I got sick. I went to sleep in one of the offices,' she recited as if by rote. 'Then I woke up and went home.'

'Succinct but hardly comprehensive,' he said gruffly, his chafing movements slowing. 'The office you chose to sleep in was mine. You were there when I staggered in from the airport. I'd spent the previous five days crisscrossing the world, flying to various meetings in Europe, the States and Asia—a pretty arduous schedule even for someone with my energy levels—and I'd had a glass or two of what I thought was innocuous punch on the way up, so by the time I saw the little brown mouse curled up on my couch I was feeling somewhat disorientated...'

He paused for so long that Harriet was forced to look at him. He was waiting for her, his face harsh and unyielding, his blue eyes steely with intent.

'I hadn't turned the lights on and I don't think you really realised who I was when you woke up—not at first, anyway, and by the time you did it didn't matter. The details are a bit blurry because I was as close to drunk as I've ever been, but I remember you talking about what your fiancé had done to you and you were crying, so I lay down beside you and put my arms around you. You seemed so small and delicate and helpless, so unlike the brisk, capable Miss Smith that I had always thought could cope with anything...'

His even delivery faltered and he looked uncomfortable and, yes, faintly ashamed. 'You were soft and trembling, you wanted to be comforted, and the comforting turned to kissing and the kissing to touching and you were so warm and so eager that one thing led to another—'

'"One thing led to another"?' Her nails curved into her palms. His words painted a picture of her practically seducing him. She would never have dared do anything like that, surely, no matter how drunk or delirious she had been? Not the mousy, conventional little thing she had then been, not with the cool and aloof Marcus Fox...in his *office*, for goodness' sake!

'We made love, Harriet.' When he saw her eyes darken in instant rejection he abandoned the pretty euphemism and elaborated, 'And yes, it was full sexual intercourse. We both had an orgasm.'

The raw, uncompromising statement was like a slap in the face. Harriet felt her cheeks sting and pulled her hands away from his to press them over the mortified flesh. She felt blistered all over with embarrassment. Suddenly it seemed all too horribly possible, especially when she thought about her recent sense of unease whenever she visited Marcus's office, her acute awareness of him, the disturbingly erotic dreams she had been having in the last few months...

'Afterwards you fell asleep again and I slipped out to make sure Security was tracking down the idiot who spiked the punch, and helping everyone get home. When I got back you were gone.'

'Why didn't you *say* something later?' she cried.

'I did try, but you seemed to have no idea what I was talking about. It was pretty obvious that as far as you were concerned it never happened—'

'Maybe it didn't,' she said desperately.

Pride hardened into hauteur on the stern face. 'Why would I lie? Believe me, it's not something I'm very proud of—taking sexual advantage of a woman who was to all intents and purposes helpless.' He stretched an arm along the back of the couch behind Harriet's platinum head, causing the top of his robe to gape further. 'The only redeeming feature is that at least we gave each other pleasure. I remember it was deliciously slow and sweet— a sort of innocent fumbling in the dark, almost as if we were both virgins—'

'I don't want to *know*!' She clapped her hands from her cheeks to her ears, but she could still hear his awful revelations.

'You can see what a dilemma I was in. Did I press the issue and possibly cause you more trauma, or leave you in blissful ignorance? A psychiatrist friend of mind said that if you genuinely had no recollection or you'd subconsciously blanked it out then I'd be better to let sleeping dogs lie...unless you started showing aberrant behaviour that could possibly be attributed to re-surfacing memory—'

'You consulted a *psychiatrist*?' Harriet squeaked.

'Only very informally...I never mentioned your name,' he said gravely, absently winding one of her curls around his finger. 'I was worried about you. I could see that you were in something of an emotionally fragile state. I felt I owed it to you to establish some kind of watching brief over you.'

Harriet sat straighter, so that her curls slipped beyond the reach of his toying hand.

'Watching brief?' Something occurred to her that made every cell in her body cringe. 'I suppose you mean this whole business about Nicola's job and me taking her under my wing was another one of your set-ups?' she said hoarsely.

'Of course not, although I think Nicola was more concerned with worming her way into the insurance business than rebelling against being at school. She just doesn't want to go on to university. I guess the last few weeks have shown she's willing to come in on the ground floor, so we'll have to see.'

Harriet relaxed fractionally. So *that* was what the girl had been up to in her demure but determined way!

'It was a very convenient way for you to spy on me, though, wasn't it?' she said, unwilling to let go of her suspicions.

'Very, but I didn't create the opportunity, I just took advantage of it,' he said with a clipped precision that suggested he objected to the slur on his honour. 'I probably would have asked you to take on the task of monitoring Nicola anyway; you were the natural choice. Of course I didn't realise how critical my intervention in your affairs was going to turn out to be...'

He leaned towards her and picked up the hand she had clenched in her lap.

'You can relax now, Harriet. You don't have to run wild in an attempt to prove to yourself how shameless and wicked and promiscuous you are. We both know you're none of those things. That was just a role created by your guilty subconscious. But you have nothing to feel guilty about. Our brief encounter may have been unwise, but it certainly wasn't sordid—or in any way promiscuous. So, you see, now you can go back to being yourself again.'

Harriet had listened with rising indignation. 'Brief encounter'? He made it sound as if they had merely shaken hands! They had *made love,* for goodness' sake. Been as intimate as it was possible for a man and woman to be. Well, if he could shrug it off so casually, so could she! she thought grimly.

She stood up, and he stood up with her, almost rocking back on his heels as she told him fiercely, 'Thank you, but you can keep your pompous, amateur psychiatric evaluations to yourself! You needn't flatter yourself that the way I act has *anything* to do with you, subconsciously or otherwise!'

He thrust his head forward aggressively. 'Don't be absurd; of course it has. I could practically taste your embarrassment a few moments ago. You were shocked by the thought of yourself casually sleeping with me. It goes against the grain, doesn't it, to hold yourself so lightly? How do you think you're going to feel about yourself if you do it on a regular basis?'

'At least next time it might be interesting enough for me to remember it for more than five minutes,' she said snidely. 'You know what they say—if you don't at first succeed, try, try, try again!'

His nostrils flared. 'Is that an invitation?'

She smiled provocatively and posed with her hands on her narrow hips, her shoulders leaning forward to emphasise her breasts, her eyes half-closed—a parody of a Marilyn Monroe pose that she had practised in the mirror. 'Do you want it to be, honey?'

He looked as savage as a man could look in a bathrobe. 'If you want to know what a *memorable* one-night stand feels like I'd be delighted to oblige.'

'But that would make it a two-night stand,' she pointed out with a toss of her head, exhilarated by his show of temper and knowing that his threat was an empty one. He was too fastidious, too much of a gentleman to let her goad him into treating her like an easy lay, especially with the smirch she had put on his much valued sense of honour at New Year so fresh in his mind.

'Chickening out already, Harriet?'

She would have looked down her small, straight nose at him if he hadn't been taller than she was. Instead she gave him an insulting once-over. 'One night? No strings? Wham-bam, thank you, Marcus?'

He gritted his teeth. 'If you're sure that's what you want.'

'That's exactly what I want!' she declared, wondering what would happen if she told him that a thousand and one nights and chains of steel were more in line with her desires.

'Fine!'

'Fine!' she echoed triumphantly. Now was the time to call his bluff. She batted her eyelashes at him. 'Shall we start here, or in the bedroom?'

His wolfish smile gave her a nasty shock. 'Oh, let's do the thing properly. A night you asked for and a night you'll get. With daylight saving I calculate that there are currently ten hours of darkness and we both have to be at work in—' he consulted his watch '—roughly eight. I don't want to short-change you.... Look, I'm afraid

I'm tied up for the next few days, so shall we say sunset on Sunday.'

Ten hours! Harriet tried not to let the thrill of shock show through her expression of careless indifference. *Ten hours?*

'Fine,' she said defiantly, clinging to the reckless certainty that he was merely trying to humiliate her into backing down before he did, to force her to admit that he was right and she was wrong. Never! She was going to win this game of brinkmanship and demonstrate once and for all that the new Harriet Smith was every bit her own person, not merely a hollow receptacle for the old Harriet's fears!

'Fine.' His defiance was every bit as razor-sharp as hers. 'I'll expect you here about eight, then.'

He escorted her politely to the door and with every step Harriet expected him to growl that enough was enough. She was in the hall, walking away, when she finally heard him break.

'Oh, Harriet?'

She spun round in relief, a tiny smile of triumph that she was helpless to hide playing insolently around her mouth.

'Yes, Marcus?' she said sweetly. 'Did you forget something?'

He was leaning against the doorway, his blue gaze burning with controlled rage. 'Just to warn you not to expect dinner. All you're getting from me is sex. I don't intend to waste a single minute of our one-night stand on anything as mundane as food...'

CHAPTER NINE

FOR the next three days Harriet was in a fog of distraction, desperately seeking to reconstruct the events of New Year's Eve from the fragments floating around in her brain. At the same time she was dreading Marcus's inevitable phone call to call off their infamous one-night stand.

The saner side of her hoped that when it came she would quietly agree with him that their game the other night had got way out of hand, apologise, and forget the whole ignominious affair.

The mad, reckless side urged her to seize the day and slam the receiver down in his ear and to glory in the wicked consequences.

At eight o'clock on Sunday, still having heard nothing, Harriet walked up to Marcus's apartment in a fever of excitement and trepidation, dressed ambiguously in a demure cream silk top and black velvet miniskirt which perfectly expressed the dichotomy of her feelings.

The trepidation vanished when she saw his expression—harsh and unsmiling.

It wasn't the face of conciliation. He was still implacably set on teaching her a punishing lesson on the dangers of casual sex. But Harriet didn't care. She wanted this one night with him more than she had wanted anything in her life. Because one night was all she had. No future, she had promised herself. Only the present.

'You can leave your clothes on the chair.'

Marcus closed the door with a decisive click and strolled past Harriet, indicating the tall, ladder-backed

162

chair that stood against the wall where the tiles of the entranceway gave way to the pale blue carpet of his lounge.

Harriet gave a nervous laugh, smoothing her palms down the side-seams of her skirt as she followed him. He was wearing the same dark blue robe that he had worn the other night. She had dressed up for the occasion and he hadn't bothered to dress at all. With a jolt she realised that he had intended it as a deliberate insult.

'Aren't you even going to offer me a drink first?' she asked coquettishly.

Her stomach, which had been a trifle unsettled over the past couple of weeks, no doubt as a result of the stress and excitement of embarking on her reckless crusade, cramped violently as he drawled, 'Why? This isn't a seduction. You're here for sex, Harriet, not the trappings of romance.' And he flicked a switch, causing the lights in the lounge to spring from soft dimness to full illumination.

'Well?' he asked as she hovered in the doorway, his eyes crawling insolently over her clothes. 'Aren't you going to take them off? Or do you want me naked first?'

His hands went to loosen his belt and Harriet let out an unknowing squeak. His hands froze.

'What did you say?'

Harriet licked her lips. She hadn't realised that it was going to be so difficult to be brazen in the face of his insolence. 'Nothing. I—you—why don't we talk a little first...?'

He folded his arms across his chest in the classic posture of male contempt. 'What about—*ma'am*?'

Wham bam! He was still unwilling to relinquish his anger.

Harriet's chin went up. Her hands reached for the buttons of her tunic blouse and she gave him a wilful, wild-child smile.

'Why, about your preferences, of course. Since I don't remember last time, you'll have to tell me what you like and don't like...'

As she undid the buttons their eyes clashed in silent battle. Excitement fountained inside her as she watched him struggle to maintain his arrogant pose. So he thought he was teaching her a lesson, did he? Maybe it was she who would be the teacher!

In the hush the whisper of silk seemed loud in her ears as the sleeveless tunic floated to the floor, leaving her bare to the waist except for the bronze satin underwired bra that lifted her small breasts into surprising prominence.

He didn't take his eyes off her face.

'I *prefer* you naked,' he said, in an affectedly bored tone that made the blood rush through her veins as she obediently unzipped her skirt with fingers that she hoped he couldn't see were shaking and shimmied her hips to let it fall around her ankles.

Harriet stepped out of the circle of black velvet and kicked it away, conscious of the sheer provocation of the careless gesture. The bronze satin bikini panties and suspender belt shone like gilded metal in the bright overhead light. Nude-coloured stockings faintly dusted with glitter encased her legs. Harriet's outer clothing might have been equivocal. Her underwear was not.

She watched Marcus's arms fall to his sides as his eyes swept over her. She couldn't believe that he wasn't sharing her electrifying excitement.

She had to believe it, though, when he turned away and walked over to the couch, sprawling casually down onto it, swinging his legs to the cushions, raising one knee so that the robe parted, revealing the length of finely furred legs almost to the apex of his thighs. The thick towelling defied any attempt to judge his arousal and there was no indication of it in his voice as he studied her for a moment and then said bluntly, 'Very titillating, my dear, but that's not what I ordered. Be a good girl and take it all off so we can get down to business.'

'My dear'. It made her sound like someone's maiden aunt. So why, in the next breath, had he striven to make her feel like a prostitute?

Because that was his plan, she realised. And Marcus Fox always stuck to a plan until someone more determined than he came along to unstick it.

Harriet bit her lip and reached around her back to the fastening of her bra. There was something perversely exciting in knowing that he wasn't a willing partner in this exercise in humiliation, that he had probably told himself that he was going to be cruel to be kind!

She eased herself slowly out of the bronze satin cups and bent to peel off her panties, conscious of her breasts swaying with her movements, their soft sides brushing delicately against her inner arms, the nipples already pointed, aching and tingling with remembered pleasure.

When she straightened again she felt a sharp thrill at the savagery of his expression but when she reached for her suspenders he stopped her.

'No! Leave them on,' he said hoarsely, and she almost fainted with disappointment. He couldn't stop her, not now! He *had* to want her!

'Come here.' The order was brutal in its lack of emotion. Oh, God, had she truly disgusted him? she thought as she walked blindly towards him. Had her bold refusal to recognise any limits on her behaviour cost her even her ability to arouse his desire? It had been her only weapon against his sophisticated armoury.

He swung his feet to the floor, sitting up, as stern as a judge and executioner watching the condemned approach. Harriet almost stumbled in her high heels, her natural grace totally deserting her.

She stood before him on the spot that he had indicated, intending to suffer his cruel sexual contempt with as much dignity as she could muster.

She summoned her last reserve of courage and looked down, and the breath left her lungs in a little rush that made her light-headed. Marcus was studying the smoothness of her taut belly and the slender fragility of her hips and the dark hair that curled with a curiously tender expression. She unconsciously clenched her thighs together to contain the blossoming of moist heat in her core and he leaned forward, his nostrils flaring as if he scented her secret rush of arousal.

He lifted a hand and fingered the delicate strap of her suspender, tracing it up her thigh to the hollow of her hip where the strap joined the satin band. Then his hand drifted inwards and, to Harriet's shock, he sifted his fingers gently through the dark hair that concealed her womanhood, fluffing the luxuriant growth.

'Ah, blondie—you're completely natural where it counts, aren't you?' he said huskily, and his fingers moved against her with even greater intimacy, the tips curling up into the tiny gap at the apex of her compressed thighs, touching her with a delicacy that made her gasp and grab his wrist.

He pulled it free and put both hands on her hips, holding her firmly, his thumbs stroking the bone.

'Don't you want my fingers stroking you there, Harriet?' he asked her softly. He kissed first one hipbone, and then the other, and his hands slid around to cup her firm buttocks. 'But how do you expect me to give you pleasure, then ? Like this, perhaps...?'

He gave a soft yank, and as she fell forward he put his mouth on her where his hand had been. Harriet felt an unbelievable burst of pure, searing sensation as his tongue parted her delicate folds.

She plunged her hands into his black hair, her fingernails scraping and digging into his scalp as her back arched in a helpless spasm, pushing her against his mouth.

'Oh!' Her thighs opened to the insistent pressure of his hard knees pushing between her legs, and she gave a soft moan as his tongue stroked her over and over until she thought she would explode.

She pulled urgently at his hair, writhing and panting in his powerful grip. 'Marcus, no, please—not like this!'

He turned his cheek against her quivering belly, rubbing her with the hardness of his jaw, soothing her sensuously. 'Hush, darling, just let it happen. I know I can give you pleasure this way... I've done it before—'

'I don't want you to *give* it to me, I want us to *share*,' she protested raggedly.

His eyes were almost cerulean in their brilliant intensity as he slowly relaxed his grasp, still holding her straddled over his knees. He leaned back, resting his shoulders against the back of the couch.

'How magnanimous of you, darling,' he murmured, his eyes on her pink face as he released the tie on his bathrobe and casually flicked back the lapels, exposing the full length of his nude body.

Harriet's heart lurched up into her throat. He was beautiful! Lean and hard, his skin glossy with health, a smattering of midnight-dark hair thickening in his groin to provide the perfect frame for his proudly thrusting masculinity. If she had ever doubted his desire for her she couldn't now. The unashamed evidence before her eyes was conclusive: smooth, hard and seeming to throb visibly under her gaze of wide-eyed wonder.

As she stared he reached for an object beside him on the couch and she saw that it was a box of condoms.

'A whole box?' she blurted out inadvertently.

'I know what an insatiable lover you are,' he said gravely, and laughed as she blushed in confusion. His humour was unexpected and beguiling. He had fought strongly against allowing her to use him, but he had given her the victory, and now he was going to apply the same fierce dedication to making love to her as he had earlier to his resistance.

He donned the protection without the least sign of modesty or embarrassment and Harriet fleetingly compared him with Keith, who used to fumble around in the dark, as if it was an offence to his masculinity. She even suspected that Marcus lingered deliberately over the intimate task, enjoying having her watching him touch himself, heightening their anticipation of the pleasure to come.

'Next time you can do it for me,' he promised huskily, and with a stunningly swift movement caught hold of her ribcage, his thumbs curving up under her breasts as he pulled her down on her knees to straddle his lap, arching his hips so that he slid smoothly inside her in the same fluid motion.

'Oh!' Harriet's hand spread across his chest as she felt him take a heaving breath and arch up again, pushing deeper, tighter, a huge, hard invasion of heat that made her instinctively grip his hips with her knees and rock forward, flexing her inner muscles around him. All her concentration was focused inwards, to that wonderful, unparalleled sensation of heat inside her. The disquieting feeling of incompleteness that had haunted her for so long was gone, and she felt a great welling of vibrant joy.

Marcus groaned and tipped his head back against the couch, his eyes closed, his face in a rictus of pleasure, his throat rippling as he swallowed convulsively.

'Don't move.' This time she knew that his grating harshness wasn't anger, it was rigid self-restraint. She obeyed, her bottom settling on his iron thighs. After a few moments of absolute stillness Marcus lifted his head and gave her a lazy smile that made her toes curl in her black shoes.

'What now, Mr Fox?' she teased him throatily.

'Now?' His hands swept down her sides and over her stockings to the knees that were wedged against his hips, and then slowly followed the same course back again.

'Now, Miss Smith, we stay like this for the next ten hours.'

She quaked with delight and laughter at the thought. 'But what if I want to move?' she asked, squirming with mock innocence.

'Why, then I suppose I'll have to do this...' His hands tangled in her suspenders, holding them as if they were reins, tightly controlling the movements of her lower body as he bent his head and began to make lavish love to her acutely sensitive breasts, her hips beginning a slow, rhythmic ride that long minutes afterwards sent Harriet shooting to the stars...

Later, when Harriet tried to count up how many times they'd made love, she got lost somewhere in the move between the lounge and the bedroom. Suffice it to say that when she woke in the morning next to Marcus she felt deliciously exhausted and unutterably contented.

Still in a half-waking state, she stretched, sensuously enjoying the slide of the satin sheets against her bare skin, and reached out to reassure herself that her erotic fantasy was really true. Her hand bumped against a hard hip and her groping finger brushed against a shaft of satiny steel that she was tempted to explore.

'Uh-uh.' Her hand was caught and firmly placed back on her own stomach. 'Your time is up, Miss Smith. Now etiquette requires you to pay a gracious compliment to your latest sexual conquest and make a discreet disappearance from his life.'

Harriet's heavy eyes flew open and she found herself looking directly up into Marcus's face. He was propped on his side on the wide, disordered bed, looking disgustingly bright and bushy-tailed for a man who had spent the night steeped in dissipation. The reports about his energy had obviously not been exaggerated. In contrast Harriet felt heavy and lethargic, her brain thick and turgid.

He watched as she slowly absorbed the impact of his words and remembered . . .

She began to rise in panic, holding the blue satin sheet bunched over her breasts, and he laid a gentle hand on her shoulder, stilling her against the soft pillows.

'If that's what you want, Harriet.'

She opened her mouth and he put his warm palm over it and continued, 'Because I think you must know by now it's not what *I* want.' His eyes darkened. 'One night isn't enough to be enough, is it, Harriet?'

No, she realised in despair, it wasn't. 'How much is enough?' she asked warily, her words muffled by his hand.

'How long is a piece of string?' he murmured, removing his hand warily from her mouth, and Harriet licked her lips, finding curious reassurance in his familiar taste. 'What do you say? Shall we take each day as it comes?' he asked.

It sounded like a leaf from Harriet's book of philosophy. She wasn't so sure about it any more, but if she could control the relationship, set the rules, then why shouldn't she share his bed again and again, letting him transport her to that wonderful other world where there was no pain, no hurt, no lasting sorrow...?

'You mean an affair?' she said bluntly.

'If that's what you want to call it,' he said, brushing the hair back from her temples.

'No strings?'

'Not unless you want them.'

She wouldn't, she told herself. No more than he.

'And my hair stays blonde,' she said fiercely.

'Of course,' he agreed glibly. His eyelids drooped. 'After all, I do have the brunette version of you available for my private pleasure.'

She dragged her pillow out from under her head and hit him in the face with it. He laughed and rose, ripping the sheets off her body and rolling her unceremoniously out of his bed.

'Come on; you're going to be late for work if you linger with your lover, and your boss might take you to task. Will cereal and juice and toast be enough for you, or would you like me to scramble you some eggs?'

Mmm, she could get used to such pampering, she thought later as she licked the marmalade from her sticky fingers at his dining-room table. She caught Marcus watching her over the top of his coffee-cup and cheekily poked her tongue out at him, but he didn't smile.

'I think you should make an appointment to see your doctor today,' he said with brooding quietness. 'That is, if you haven't already consulted him.'

She frowned and put down her last piece of toast, suddenly feeling unpleasantly overfull. 'It's a her. And why should I have?'

Her brow cleared as she realised what he was delicately trying to suggest. 'I'm not quite as irresponsible as you seem to think. I have condoms in my purse and, since I plan to always have my partners practise safe sex,

I decided it wasn't necessary to arrange any other form of contraception.'

His eyes narrowed at her use of both the plural and the future tense. 'Any woman who plans to become sexually active should have a thorough check-up, just to make sure there aren't any existing problems that could flare up,' he said, adding wryly, 'Especially if the love-making is frequent, prolonged and vigorous.'

He smiled behind his cup as Harriet's air of sophistication collapsed and her cheeks went cherry-red. 'Yes, well, I'll make an appointment with Dr Baker some time this week,' she said hurriedly, fussing with her hair in order to avoid his amused eyes.

'If you want me to make love to you tonight you'll see her today,' he repeated firmly.

A little thrill ran down her spine before she remembered, 'Tonight is my French class.'

'What time does it start?'

'Eight o'clock.'

Nightfall. Their eyes met in perfect accord on the thought.

'And when does it finish?'

'Not until half past ten,' she said wistfully, peeping at him through her naked brown lashes.

'Mmm...that only leaves us seven and a half hours in bed,' he mused silkily. 'Hardly time to warm ourselves up.'

Harriet was already warm all over. 'I'll make sure I see Dr Baker at lunchtime,' she vowed fervently, and he leaned back and laughed at her expression.

'And I'll go home for dinner with Nicola and see her off to bed before I come back into town.'

'Will—will you tell her where you're going?'

'Yes. Does that bother you?'

It shouldn't have, given the girl's previously stated approval, but it did...a little. However, not enough to outweigh the selfish joy of having Marcus to herself.

'No. I just hope...' Harriet hesitated and he raised his eyebrows '...that she doesn't mention it to her grandmother,' she finished in a little rush. 'She told me that Mrs Jerome has already called three times since she went on holiday and has...well...'

His mouth quirked. '"Interrogated her" is the phrase I think you're looking for. I think Susan may already be aware that I've seen much more of you than I have of Lynne since she left. Nicola does tend to pepper her conversation with your name.'

'Oh, dear,' she murmured with a tiny glimmer of smugness.

'Actually I spoke to Susan myself yesterday and reassured her that you weren't a torrid blonde floozy,' he said drily. 'She's arriving back today, but, don't worry, I'll protect you.'

Several hours later she wasn't the least impressed with the level of Marcus's protection as she reeled out of Dr Baker's clinic after losing her lunch in the rest room.

Pregnant!

Harriet was three months pregnant!

Since New Year's Eve she had been blithely walking around with her lover's baby growing inside her! *Marcus Fox's* baby. Nicola's stepbrother or sister!

Collapsing into the Porsche, Harriet leant her clammy forehead on the leather steering wheel. She had never thought to ask if Marcus had used a condom all those months ago. She had just assumed that he would have been his normal over-responsible self. But of course he hadn't been...neither of them had been in any state to consider the intrinsic biological purpose of their actions.

She had been slightly embarrassed in the doctor's surgery that she had not recognised the changes in her body for what they were. But then, how could she have, when she hadn't even known that pregnancy was a possibility? It all seemed so obvious now—her unpredictable stomach upsets combined with a greatly increased appetite and odd food cravings, her wild swings of emotion, her pleasing weight gain over the past few weeks and the tenderness of her breasts... although the latter she had attributed to her growing sexual awareness of Marcus. She just hadn't realised how big it would grow, she thought hysterically.

'But I can't be—I'm still having my periods!' Harriet had cried when both she and the doctor had been astonished by the result of the routine pelvic examination.

'You're definitely pregnant,' Dr Baker had said, 'but we'll do the test just to remove all doubt.' And while they had sat and waited for the result she had told Harriet that it wasn't unusual for some women to have quite heavy spotting in the first few months of their pregnancy.

'Have you noticed your periods being much lighter than usual?'

'Well, maybe, yes... a little... some,' Harriet conceded. 'But I thought that was because I was depressed and under a lot of emotional stress.'

'Mmm, that's why I want to get you onto an iron supplement right away,' Dr Baker said. 'After your father died you let yourself get quite run-down, and for the baby's sake you need to build your condition back up as quickly as possible. But I'm leaping ahead of myself. I'm presuming here that you want to continue the pregnancy?'

Harriet put her hands over her stomach and uttered instinctively, 'Oh, yes,' and then more strongly as the implications hit her, 'Oh, *yes!*'

New life. She was carrying a new *life*. A part of herself and therefore a part of the family she had lost. Her baby would carry some of their genetic characteristics, creating another bridge between the past and the future. The circle of life was complete . . . birth, death, rebirth. Yes, Harriet too would die in her turn, but her baby would live and grow and give birth to new generations . . .

In six months' time she would be part of a *family* again, she realised in wonder.

'Now, are you sure of your dates?' Dr Baker asked briskly when the confirmation came through from the clinic laboratory. 'From the palpitation I did during the examination you seem to be rather large for three months.'

'It was definitely New Year's Eve,' said Harriet weakly.

Dr Baker smiled knowingly. 'Ah. A celebration baby.'

A celebration baby. It certainly was, but not in the way that Dr Baker had meant it.

Harriet drove the Porsche very carefully on the way back to the office. She wondered numbly if Porsche made a child-restraint she could fit to her car. Thank goodness she hadn't blown all of her inheritance yet!

It wasn't until she walked back into the file room and saw Nicola that her bubble of self-absorption burst and she remembered that there was someone else with a vested interest in the life that her body contained.

Marcus! Oh, God, what was *Marcus* going to say? They had just agreed to start a no-strings affair and now she was going to land him with a baby!

Harriet slumped over her desk, burying her face in her hands. She felt sick. If she told him that she was pregnant he would probably feel compelled to take responsibility for her and her baby. He would order her about, he would try to curtail her freedom, he might even . . . God forbid . . . want to marry her. No, not *want*.

He would feel that he had no choice, honourable man that he was.

But there was no choice for her now either, with a baby on the way. She couldn't run away from a helpless child for fear of loving it too much. For the baby's sake she would *have* to make an emotional investment in the future.

But not with Marcus. He made it clear that he enjoyed her body and her company, but he had never once tried to lay claim to her emotions, and he kept his own cloaked in a reserve that was difficult to penetrate. If she was voluntarily going to re-enter the real world of real relationships, with all their potential joys and tragedies, then she would find a man who would accept his share of the burdens of loving...

'Harriet? Are you all right? You look awful. Did something happen at the doctor's?'

She became aware of Nicola, crouched beside her chair, peering anxiously at her tormented expression.

Harriet straightened like a jack-in-a-box. 'No, no, I'm fine,' she said shrilly, giving Nicola a huge, toothpaste smile.

Nicola smiled back uncertainly. 'Good, because Daddy wants to see you. He phoned a few minutes ago and asked if you would go up as soon as you got back from lunch.'

Oh, God! She couldn't ignore the summons. He would get suspicious, especially knowing where she had been. If only she had had more time to think, to adjust...

It seemed to Harriet that everyone in the hallways and in the lift was glancing at her mid-section and speculating about her guilty secret, and by the time she reached Marcus's office her nerves were wound as tight as a drum.

When she went in he was standing behind his desk, hands in his pockets, frowning at nothing in particular.

He hurriedly withdrew his hands. 'Harriet! How did the visit to the doctor go?'

'Fine,' she said cheerfully, fully prepared for that one.

'Mmm.' He gave her a considering look. 'I've just spoken to Nicola—I was wondering where you were. She said you came back a little late, and seemed rather pale.'

'Uh, did she?' Drat! She hadn't been prepared for that. Her eyes slid away from Marcus's and she pretended to flick a speck off her black leather skirt. 'I got caught in traffic.' She could feel the warmth under her collar and hoped it didn't show.

His cool blue eyes sharpened. 'You would tell me, wouldn't you, if something was wrong?'

The back of her neck got hotter. 'Of course I would,' she lied, with a beatific smile.

He prowled around the edge of his desk and hitched his hip to sit on the corner nearest her, his free-swinging leg almost brushing her skirt.

'Good...good. Because that's important—that we trust each other sufficiently to be honest about ourselves,' he said. 'That we don't feel constrained to hold things back for fear of being hurt or embarrassed.'

Harriet's guilt grew to crippling proportions. Would he be hurt or embarrassed to learn of his impending fatherhood? He surely wouldn't be as joyous as Harriet had been after the first instant of horror. He had a fifteen-year-old daughter, for goodness' sake; he had been through it all before. Another baby, especially an illegitimate one, would be seen as a tiresome complication rather than a miraculous gift of love. She was right not to tell him about it yet, to wait until she had formulated a plan for her and the baby's future that would be proof against all the pressures he was sure to bring to bear on her to conform to *his* plans...

She mumbled a vague agreement and he picked up her hand and rested it on his knee for a moment, smiling at her, before he turned it over and idly traced the life-line in her palm.

'What did you call me up here for?' she asked desperately, when it seemed that he wasn't going to say anything else.

'Perhaps I just wanted to see you?' His finger slid into the crease between her thumb and forefinger and stroked back and forth—a simple, innocent gesture that seemed unbearably erotic.

'Why?' She could feel the familiar tingling in her breasts—breasts which soon would give loving nourishment to his child.

'Do I have to have a reason?' he said huskily, pulling her slowly towards him.

'Usually you have a reason for everything you do.'

He stroked her cheek. 'How boring of me.' He fingered a button of her white, mannish shirt until it slid open, and moved on down to the next one. 'I have to try and be less logical on occasion.'

'Marcus, what do you think you're doing?' she asked as he flicked open another button to reveal a peek of lace.

'Just browsing, darling.' When he said 'darling' like that in that dark, velvety voice, it sent shivers up her spine. A person very much loved; if only he was using the word literally, rather than as a casual endearment. 'Would you like to make love?'

'Here?' She was shocked to her toes by his unconventional suggestion. 'But this is your office!'

He lifted her hand to his mouth and bit into the succulent base of her thumb. 'It worked for us once before,' he murmured, his blue eyes dilating.

And *how* it had worked! She glanced involuntarily at the couch where her baby had been conceived.

'Marcus, for goodness' sake, don't be silly!' It was a plea she'd never thought she'd hear herself make. 'It's broad daylight,' she added irrelevantly as he slid his hand inside her loosened shirt to cup her lace-covered breast, squeezing it very gently, and fondling her in a way that made her sway bonelessly towards him.

'It'll be a new experience for you, then,' he promised, standing up and taking her fully into his arms. 'You like new experiences, Harriet,' he reminded her, and kissed the next protest from her mouth with consummate skill.

'Marcus...' She put the arms that had intended to push him away around his hard waist. If she still found him this irresistible, how would she ever persuade herself to let him go?

He gave a grunt of satisfaction and shrugged out of his jacket, letting it fall to the floor. His hand curved over her leather-clad bottom, massaging it lightly as he nudged her backwards towards the couch, kissing her all the way, and she found herself helplessly murmuring his name again.

'Yes, Harriet?' His hand was under her bra now, finding a throbbing nipple.

'Marcus, we can't do this.' She hoped she sounded stern.

'Why not?' He sat on the couch with her, his mouth warm and encouraging on hers. 'Don't you like it?' His hand began to creep up under the hem of her skirt.

Her thoughts were scattering. 'Yes, but—'

'Don't you want me?' He abandoned her mouth and kissed her throat, her bared collar-bone, and nibbled sensuously around the stud in her ear.

Harriet tilted her head to give him better access. 'Yes, but—'

'Did the doctor forbid you?' he asked slyly, his thumb rubbing the stiff little peak of her breast.

She moaned. 'No, but—'

'But what? What is it that you're running from this time, Harriet?' he coaxed in a throaty murmur as he pushed her onto her back and came over her. 'You can tell me. You can trust me with all your little secrets, darling. I'm the absolute soul of discretion . . .'

'But *I'm* not,' she burst out. 'I'm wildly *in*discreet. It's no use; I can't be the kind of mistress you want. I'm not cut out for discreet affairs. I can't bear to hold my feelings inside the way you do. I might have been like that once, but I can't go back to a life like that. I don't want to have to pretend; I don't want to have to be passionate in private but prim and proper in public. You wouldn't be able to take me anywhere with you; I'd be a public relations disaster, always embarrassing you with emotional displays. And . . . I'm . . . and I'm . . .' The jagged words that might deliver the final push to send him away stuck dangerously in her throat.

'And what? What else are you, Harriet?' he asked harshly, in contrast to the silky smoothness of a few moments before.

'And I'm in love with you,' she admitted in a shattered voice. She lay still, exhausted by the small, violent storm, waiting for him to laugh, or withdraw, or, worse, say something *kind* . . .

He did none of those things. He braced himself on his strong arms, looked calmly down at her turbulent face and said, 'Well, it certainly took you long enough to work that out, darling.'

'*What?*'

He put his face down, his nose an inch away from hers, and said with banked fierceness, 'What do you think I've been doing with you all this time, if not waiting for you to come to me of your own free will? You complain *you* don't have any freedom!' He laughed through his teeth. 'For God's sake, I've had you haunting me for *months* . . . wanting to see you again, to talk to you, to touch you, feeling that I didn't have the right after what I'd done.

'It was a vicious circle...feeling guilty for wanting you, watching you, wanting you even more...feeling even guiltier. Waiting, plotting, planning for the most auspicious time to edge a little closer without frightening the timid prey into taking flight...only to have you suddenly take off in my face and buzz around in and out of my reach like a demented honey-bee.'

He put a finger on the lower lip of her gaping mouth and held it open, so that he could sip the sweet nectar there. 'And then,' he said huskily, 'when I finally had you exactly where I wanted you—*then* you wanted to treat me like a casual *fling*!'

There was a knock at the door and he turned his head to yell hoarsely, 'Open that door, whoever you are, and you're fired!'

The door opened instantly, and Susan Jerome marched briskly in, leaving the door swinging wide behind her. In the outer office a group of suited executives did a violent double take at the sight of their dishevelled chairman sprawled on his office couch with an equally rumpled companion.

'*Marcus!* Don't tell me you *still* can't keep your hands off the girl!' his mother-in-law thundered. 'Can't you at least exercise *some* self-restraint? If *this* is the way you two *carry on* when you're alone together I'm *surprised* that *either* of you manages to get any *work* done at all!'

The censorious outburst, bristling with outraged italics, was thoroughly justified. This time there was absolutely no doubt as to what she had interrupted.

Marcus flopped back on the couch with a loud groan, placing his arm across his eyes, while Harriet hurriedly scrambled off, buttoning her shirt and trying to find the shoes that had dropped off her feet. When the group of young executives riveted outside the door fanned back to their various departments the gossip would spread through the building like wildfire. All she could think of was the damage that this would do to Marcus's reputation, and how much he would hate being the subject of cheap jokes amongst his employees...*especially* blonde jokes!

'Mrs Jerome—uh—I know you'll want to be the first to officially congratulate us!' she said loudly, tucking her shirt back into her skirt. There was a strangled sound from the couch behind her, but Harriet held her head high under the bullet-grey stare. She didn't want Marcus to lose his mother-in-law's respect either. 'Marcus and I have just become *engaged,*' she said in ringing tones.

At that moment Clare Broadbent leaned apologetically into the room and hurriedly pulled the door closed, shutting out their avid audience.

'I'm afraid that we got carried away in the heat of the moment,' Harriet said unblushingly to Susan Jerome in her normal voice. 'I'm sure, given the special circumstances, you can understand—'

'Of course she can, darling.' Marcus's arms came sliding around her waist, pulling her back hard against his supporting body. 'She remembers what it was like to be in love, don't you, Susan?'

The answer was a stiff 'harrumph'!

'Thank you for springing to my protection so recklessly, by the way, darling,' Marcus murmured into the blonde curls at the back of Harriet's head. 'I'm very flattered, and delighted to accept your very proper proposal. By way of a thank-you I hope you'll accept this wildly extravagant token of my undying respect...'

Harriet looked down as his hands fumbled at her waist and saw that he was opening a small velvet box. She gasped when she saw the blaze of diamonds inside. He stepped around in front of her and picked up her left hand, kissing it before sliding the ring on her finger.

She looked nervously at Susan Jerome, but to her surprise the woman was smiling at them rather sentimentally.

'Marcus! You know I only said that because it was the first respectable explanation I could think of on the spur of the moment,' she hissed at him.

'A meeting of minds, darling,' he agreed, preventing her frantic efforts to remove the ring by the simple expedient of interweaving his fingers with hers. Her protest died in wonder at the expression in his eyes: no restraint, no holding back, just sheer, blue, laughing joy.

'You only pre-empted me by a few minutes,' he informed her. 'I love you, Harriet, and if you think I'm letting you wriggle out of this one after the wild dance you've led me you can think again. Susan is here to help with the wedding arrangements, aren't you, Susan?'

'I told you on the phone I would,' came the tart reply. 'Although it should be a *church*. I don't approve of this *register* office business.'

'Ah, well, there could be a bit of a rush, you see, Susan. I think my fiancée might have another little announcement to make...'

Harriet, who had been dazed by the realisation that Marcus had already discussed marrying her with his mother-in-law, looked at him, doubt splintering her happiness. 'You knew about the baby?' she faltered.

'Not knew...hoped,' he said gravely. 'That's what you are to me, Harriet...all my hopes and my dreams for the future.'

And while he kissed her shocked italics richocheted around the room. 'The *poor girl* is *pregnant*? Marcus, how *could* you? Well, that *settles* it; it's the *register* office first thing in the *morning*!'

CHAPTER TEN

MARCUS FOX stood in his nineteenth-floor office, looking down with a wry twist to his mouth at the tawny blonde in the short black swing-coat cutting a swathe through the afternoon lunch crowd in Aotea Square. Causing chaos and proud of it, he thought with humorous resignation, watching the heads whip round to follow her progress across the square.

He bent his eye to the telescope in front of him and brought her into focus. She walked with a jaunty, confident stride, swaying provocatively on her high heels, her hair flirting about her shoulders with every step, the multicoloured, sun-streaked strands such a perfect blending of the most sought-after shades that it couldn't possibly be natural.

She was gathering stares all right, but most of them were for the three miniature versions of herself whom she had in tow. They stretched out to the side of her, joined hand in hand like a string of identical paper-cutout dolls, in their little black coats and patent leather shoes and baby-fair curls.

Marcus had time to sign several letters and dictate a memo before the door to his office flew open and the tribe burst in.

'Darling!' Harriet threw her arms wide in greeting and Marcus's eyebrows lifted as the buttonless black coat split open and revealed a new fire-engine-red dress. It buttoned down the front and was short and fashionably tight over her rounded breasts and slim hips, and he could feel his loins tighten involuntarily and his mouth go dry.

He swallowed and averted his eyes and saw Nicola, an elegant young lady with a sleek chignon and a power suit, as befitted a junior executive and heir to a business empire. She had strolled in behind Harriet, in time to catch his reaction, and she rolled her eyes and grinned wickedly at his expression.

He looked down at his four-year-old identical triplet daughters, Lizzie, Jessica and Kate, and saw them stretching their arms wide like their mother, china-blue eyes pleading for Daddy to pick them up and give them a hug. He did so with an enthusiasm that made them giggle, then he picked up Harriet and spun her around, making her coat swirl out like a cape.

'Hello, Mrs Fox. Did I ever tell you how much trouble I went through to get you?' he murmured against her mouth.

'Frequently!' she laughed, her sunny eyes warm and unshadowed, her softly tinted blonde hair brushing against his face as she returned his kiss. 'Have I been worth it?'

He looked from her to the triplets, to Nicola, and back to Harriet again.

'Every single grey hair.'

She laughed again, and stroked the midnight-dark head, now liberally streaked with silver. 'That's good. Because... remember the office New Year's Eve party last year?'

'Vividly,' he said with a sultry smile. 'What—?' He stopped as he saw her impish look, and she was enchanted to see him flush with pride and pleasure. 'You're pregnant again?'

She nodded. 'Susan's ordered me to have a boy this time.'

'Or three,' he added wryly, and hugged her to his overflowing heart.

And Harriet closed her eyes, revelling in the knowledge that the circle of love they had created together would only strengthen and grow more precious with the years...

by
Miranda Lee

Complete stories of love down under that
you'll treasure forever.

Watch for:

#1855 *A WEEKEND TO REMEMBER*

It was only a little white lie...but before she knew it,
Hannah had pretended she was Jack Marshall's fiancée.
How long would it be before Jack regained his memory?

Available in December wherever
Harlequin books are sold.

HARLEQUIN PRESENTS®

ATR1

HARLEQUIN  PRESENTS®

#1854 A BABY FOR CHRISTMAS
by Anne McAllister

Years ago Piran St. Just had rejected Carly's innocent infatuation. But when Piran finds a helpless baby abandoned on his doorstep Carly wonders if this child will bring them together at last....

Will it be

THIS TIME, FOREVER

Harlequin Presents—the best has just gotten better!

Available in December wherever Harlequin books are sold.

Look us up on-line at: http://www.romance.net

TTF6

1997
Reader's Engagement Book
A calendar of important dates
and anniversaries for readers to use!

Informative and entertaining—with notable
dates and trivia highlighted throughout the year.

Handy, convenient, pocketbook size to help you
keep track of your own personal important dates.

Added bonus—contains $5.00 worth of coupons
for upcoming Harlequin and Silhouette books.
This calendar more than pays for itself!

 Available beginning in November at
your favorite retail outlet.

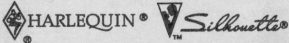

Merry Christmas, Baby!

A romantic collection filled with the magic
of Christmas and the joy of children.

SUSAN WIGGS, Karen Young and
Bobby Hutchinson bring you Christmas wishes,
weddings and romance, in a charming
trio of stories that will warm up your
holiday season.

MERRY CHRISTMAS, BABY! also contains
Harlequin's special gift to you—a set of
FREE GIFT TAGS included in every book.

Brighten up your holiday season with
MERRY CHRISTMAS, BABY!

Available in November at
your favorite retail store.

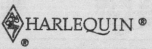

HARLEQUIN ®

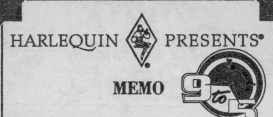

HARLEQUIN PRESENTS®

MEMO

To: The Reader
From: The Editor at Harlequin Presents
Subject: #1853 MISTLETOE MAN
by Kathleen O'Brien

Three years ago Daniel Blaisdell fired Lindsay because she dared suggest there was more to life than business—like falling in love. Now Lindsay has a major deal to negotiate with her ex-boss....

P.S. Harlequin Presents—the best has just gotten better! Available in December wherever Harlequin books are sold.

P.P.S. Look us up on-line at: http://www.romance.net